Agents and Legends

This is a work of fiction. Similarities to real people, places, or events are entirely coincidental.

AGENTS & LEGENDS

First edition. March 6, 2024.

Copyright © 2024 Juan Pastorelli.

ISBN: 979-8224679317

Written by Juan Pastorelli.

Table of Contents

by
Juan Pastorelli

Dedicated to my loving supportive wife,
my imaginative and crazy boys,
And my God and Savior

CHAPTER I

Arlington, TX

The limousine cruised to a stop in front of one of the elegantly clad servants. The man stepped forward to receive the guests as expected but did not approach the vehicle. Propriety dictated he wait until the chauffeur let the guests out or they step out themselves. He did, however, listen for voices from the interior.

"You pick now to do this?" A man's voice, clear and gruff. "You look fine, great, beautiful, look, we're here already..."

"Party. Isn't that what you said? A big party. This is hardly a party, it's a huge gala at an expensive mansion with a bunch of rich people!" An exasperated female voice that nonetheless sounded appealing. The footman perked up, anxious to put a pretty face to the sexy voice. "I have to finish my makeup, and my hair needs teasing..."

Sigh. "I'll wait outside. I'll let them know we're here. Just...don't take too long. I can't see how much you have to do, you are absolutely gorgeous just the way you are."

A girlish giggle. "You are such a charmer! Now I remember why you're my favorite. Go on, I won't be five minutes."

"You have the corsage on, right? Do you need me to help adjust it?" More giggles and the car shifted.

"Get out of here! That's extra for you!"

The door opened and the servant snapped to attention, curious to see if the car's inhabitants were half as interesting as they sounded. He was somewhat disappointed. The man who stepped out and closed the door behind him was in his mid-forties. He was tall and slim, with a long clean-shaven face. His dark hair was still full and perfectly groomed, with silver hair at both temples. He wore a white dinner jacket on dark blue slacks and a pale blue dress shirt topped by a black striped bowtie. His eyes were active, however, scanning the area and taking in all of his surroundings. He nodded to the footman as he adjusted his cufflinks.

"Gregori Stephanos and guest. She'll...be a minute. Is that okay?"

The footman checked his clipboard and saw Gregori Stephanos, plus one, VIP Plus.

"Of course, Mr. Stephanos. That's perfectly okay. This is the receiving line, and there's still plenty of room. Your guest should have plenty of time to get even prettier." He stopped as he realized he had given himself away and blushed. "I'm sorry sir. I didn't mean to overhear..."

Gregori flashed a half smile at him and waved him quiet. "It's okay, son, We all do it, to some extent or another."

"And some of us are better at it than others," the voice in his head said.

Gregori managed to turn his laugh into a cough. He turned away from the confused young man and walked up the steps slowly, muttering to himself.

"Rosalyn, are you jealous that I didn't bring you to this thing? You know I offered. Some dinner, some dancing, schmoozing with the snobbery, maybe a little romance afterward..."

"Oh, I know all about your romance, Roman Capule." Despite the sarcastic tone, he could hear the laughter in her voice. "I think you get quite enough of that from other younger and more wide-eyed victims. Besides, you need someone to be your eyes and ears." There was a pause, and he smiled to himself.

"It's just...seriously, the girl? Her? Did you really need...her?"

"She's here to be a distraction, Rosalyn. Another tool of the trade. And I'd look out of place at an event like this without some eye candy hanging on my arm. You know as well as I do that half the old geezers here will have girls young enough to be their granddaughters. And far too many of those won't be here just as visual appeal. While she is an escort, she is here simply to make me look the part."

"I know how these things work, Roman. I've been in the business long enough. I do appreciate your discretion. But did she really have to be so...I don't know...well-rounded?"

This time Gregori, or Roman Capule as he was known to his employers, let a chuckle escape before turning it into a discreet cough.

"Again, distraction, Rosalyn my dear. It's a fact that seven out of ten men and nine out of ten women notice a large bust, especially when it's accentuated properly. And that attention could mean the difference between a mission's success and death. So yes, if having a girl with some flattering décolletage by my side will help keep me alive, then I will use it, just like any other tool in my repertoire."

"You made up those numbers."

"Regardless."

Roman reached up and adjusted his bow tie, then a thought struck him. "How's the corsage looking?"

There was a snort through the invisible earpiece. "Little Miss BBB is so busy adjusting her décolletage that it's making me dizzy. But the hidden camera is working perfectly."

"BBB?"

"Blonde Busty Bimbo."

Roman grinned and shook his head. He was about to open his mouth to retort when the limo door clicked open. The footman nearly tripped over himself sprinting to the door to help the twenty something out of the vehicle. She was pristine and flawless, more Princess Barbie and less Poor College Student Barbie. Swirling blonde locks framed her cherubic face and ruby red lips parted and gleamed in exactly the right way. She was successfully filling out a long fluttering blue lacy gown with a plunging neckline. Pinned to one of the straps was the pink and white corsage. She reached out a jewelry-laden hand (too ostentatious to be real) to Roman as she stepped forward on delicate six inch heels, the dress swirling around her.

Seeing where the bulging eyes of the footman were fixed, Roman chuckled. "This might work better than I thought. Now if only Sean Quinn is also a connoisseur."

His only answer was another derisive snort.

"Gregori Stephanos, pleased to meet you finally! I've heard all about your infamously thrilling yacht parties! Tell me, is the Duchess really as feisty drunk as they say?"

Roman stopped to greet the portly bank owner as Christy waited, hand laid gently on his arm and a luminous toothy smile pasted on her face. She was a pro at this, used to dealing with these kinds of attentions, and was able to not notice the many stares she was receiving. By day she was a college student studying to be a nurse, but by night she moonlighted as a companion to exclusive personnel...this was not the first time Roman had used her services in this capacity.

Roman, his eyes locked on Sean Quinn across the room, nonetheless played up his part as the Silver Greek, heir to a shipping fleet owned by his father and frequent thrower of yacht parties that always got broken up by the Coast Guard. He was very careful. You never knew when this identity might be needed to open a door later. It was the reason he was using it tonight for this mission.

Roman was here to get close to Sean Quinn, a reclusive tech prodigy who was throwing this ball to unveil his newest product, some drug Roman had no idea about, and didn't care. According to his employer, that unveiling could not happen. Quinn was to be silenced, in as inauspicious and quiet a way as possible. Tonight.

Roman smiled and laughed and chatted people up, never failing to introduce his companion as he skillfully led them through the room. He didn't know yet how he was going to get to Quinn and get him somewhere alone, but he would think of something. He was used to thinking up plans on the fly. After all, he had been in this business for over twenty years.

When it came to fulfilling the mission, Roman Capule considered himself the best. When he had officially retired from the agency eight years ago, only a few months had passed before he realized he had retired too early. He started freelancing, brushing up on new techniques and skills, acquiring more up-to-date tech, and getting in touch with old clients and contacts. Though he tried to keep his ethics ahead of his desire for adventure, sometimes he had to take questionable jobs to return favors or open doors. That was why he was now collaborating with his current employer, one he had worked with a few times in the past. The Robinson Estates was an independent privately owned group that was involved in making sure greedy executives and corrupt mega companies didn't stand in the way of human progress and used any means necessary to achieve that. Including using a former special agent to commit assassinations.

"So far the guest list checks out," Rosalyn's voice was crystal clear in his ear, despite the distance. She was sitting in an unmarked van several miles away, monitoring the camera on Christy's chest, his vitals through the electronic tattoo on his chest, the hidden camera in his lapel, and what she had been able to piggyback from the security feed in the mansion itself, which was considerable. She kept him apprised of the situation around him, feeding him a stream of data so he could make the split-second decisions fieldwork required him to make. He had never met her in person, as she operated exclusively for the mysterious directors of the Estates. She was one of their permanent agents, but he had never worked with a controller who was more reliably good at this job.

"Good. Keep an eye on who Quinn's talking to, I might be able to use an introduction as a segue." Roman had just introduced Christy to a couple of young men who owned beachfront property in Hawaii, knowing the three would be fully occupied with each other. He waited until he felt himself being gradually ignored, and then excused himself to fetch refreshments for the group. As he turned away, he noticed a server cutting through the crowd, and his eyebvrows creased slightly. He didn't recognize the server, and she was carrying nothing, nor was she engaging in any of hte guests.

"Hey, what do you have on hired help? Have all servers and caterers been checked out thoroughly?" His voice rumbled, the sub-dermal mike hidden in his bowtie easily picking up his voice through the chaos of the party.

"Hold please." Roman watched the server out of the corner of his eye as he walked by the refreshment table. He blinked twice, fast, and his vision telescoped and zeroed into the girl, enhancing details so he could study her better.

The girl was dressed innocuously as one of the servers; loose black slacks and a featureless white button-down shirt, but he noticed that instead of wearing the black oxfords the rest of them had on, she had dark grey slip-on sneakers. Allows for fast movement without hindrance and can be kicked off easily, he instantly analyzed. She was tall, almost as tall as him, with an athletic build. She had dark mocha skin, but he noticed her facial features betrayed some European descent. Her eyes, especially, were shards of jade, glinting hard in the light. Her thick brown wavy hair was pulled back in a bun on top of her head. She was handsome, with high cheekbones and almost classically symmetrical features but there had been no attempts to highlight and enhance and conceal with makeup and hair placement. Others still noticed, however. He saw the looks many were directing at her, especially the young men, but the diffident chill she radiated seemed to hold them back. She should've been nondescript, relatively uninteresting in a room full of the rich and beautiful, despite her own simple comeliness. But a closer inspection showed why she had set off his alarms. Her thick lips were pursed in deliberation, her stride was delicate but determined, he had already noted that unlike the other servers she carried no tray or cleaning cloths, did not pause to take any orders, and those green eyes were focused on her destination. He scanned her eyeline and cursed under his breath.

"What's wrong?"

"What's the status on that info?" he responded tersely. He reached into his pocket and pressed a combination on a small key fob. The colors in his eyes bled away, allowing him to see contours and shading. He had been hoping not to use this gadget up until later, out of fear of the security measures Quinn might have, but his instincts were screaming at him. He focused on her clothing and saw several suspicious bulges in her pants, along the thighs, and on her back. Could be, he thought grimly. Could very well be. Unconventional shapes for a normal person to be loaded down with.

"Most of the staff checks out," Rosalyn said matter-of-factly. She sensed the tension. "Two are new, however, added this morning, brought in to replace an employee who suddenly got sick. Justin Harmon is the caterer's cousin. And the other...has no records. Just a name and a social that's coming up fake. Dolores Romero. She's..."

"A woman of color, about five foot eight, black hair, green eyes, no references, no employment history?"

"Affirmative," Rosalyn's voice was tense. "What's the update, agent?"

"I think we have a second hitter. She's making a beeline straight for Quinn and not subtle about it. And it looks like she's packing. I'm intercepting. I'll have to give you a more detailed description later unless you have eyes on her from the cameras. Find out what you can ASAP. Keep an eye on Quinn, there's a chance we can salvage this, but tonight might be a bust."

Roman had already keyed the command to restore his vision to normal and was pulling away from the table, two champagne flutes in each hand. Without seeming to move deliberately or quickly, he nonetheless managed to meet up with the server, Dolores. He noted as he approached that her hand kept straying to her back, where one of the odd lumps was concealed. Her hard eyes flicked to him, questioning, but before she could do more than register his presence, he had artfully stumbled. The flutes flew through the air toward her and splashed all over her. With a gasp she stopped and gaped at him, aware of the spectacle she made, and he was pleased to see that the front of her shirt was completely soaked through. His aim was still pretty good. There was some gasps and hands raised to mouths as the elegant guests instantly drew away from the messy pair.

"Oh, OH, oh I am so sorry, that's...ugh...alcohol abuse and all that, amirite? Oh, oops, and it's getting a little risqué if you know what I mean. Getting a little PG-13 for this shindig...good thing you're wearing that tank underneath, huh? No, don't scowl, you'll get unflattering wrinkles, you're right it's not funny, here, let me help you. Put my jacket on and come with me, we gotta get that off of you and something decent in, I mean, on you, a little slip of the tongue there, pardon my smitten mouth..."

Amid the laughter and parting jabs by the festive onlookers, and more than one disappointed boo from the young men, Roman guided the girl towards one of the hallways. Keeping up a constant stream of comforting but inane talk, he and the girl exited the main room and ducked down one hallway after another, looking for a bathroom or empty room. He was pretty sure that Sean Quinn and his entourage hadn't noticed anything more unusual than the Silver Greek making his moves on another unsuspecting conquest.

The quiet voice in his ear was slightly urgent. "There's nothing in NGI on her, no record in the drivers register, and she doesn't come up in any searches. That doesn't happen, nobody is this invisible. Keep your distance, agent, this could be a trap."

Roman grunted. "Little late for that," he muttered under his breath.

The girl was flustered and off balanced. That was the only way he had been able to get her this far. But she was quickly recovering her composure, frowning at him as she tried to figure him out. His velvety hand on the small of her back was not helping, and he knew from the way she tensed as his fingers brushed up against something metal that she was about to act. He grabbed the nearest door and pushed her in, then shut it behind him. She spun away from him and her hand flew to her back, only to see the barrel of his plastic dart gun pointed at her. Her eyes flicked down at the barrel, then back up to his. A sneer crawled across her face.

"Using a gun, monster? Don't your kind usually do your dirty work au naturale?" Her accent was strong, very much like Jamaican Patois, but her enunciation was clear and concise. Her choice of words, however, baffled him. He frowned, a little confused.

"My kind? Don't they use guns in the islands?"

She was good, much better than he had anticipated, and it was the only reason why she was able to get the drop on him. As his eyes swept to the side to take in the room, she moved in that split second.

Whirling around and low, she swept one arm up and batted away the gun as her other hand whipped out what was behind her back. The ease and speed of her reaction took him by surprise as she drew the sword and slammed it into his chest.

He stared down at the empty hilt pressed against his sternum. His heart took a moment to slow down from the near spike, and he briefly wondered how that would look on Rosalyn's diagnostics. For her part, the girl's look of triumph faded into one of confusion as he refused to fall down and die.

Frowning down at the hilt, she murmured, "I thought..." but then was away again, backing up and still holding the ornate sword hilt in front of her like a weapon. Her eyes shot daggers of disgust at him.

"So is that it then? You work for him? You betray your own kind for your thirty pieces of silver? Despicable bounty hunter!" She feinted with the hilt, then reached down at her thigh, probably to remove another weapon.

As entertaining and pleasant as her voice and the exchange was, she was getting more confusing. He had taken a defensive stance when she feinted, but as she reached down he raised the gun again and pointed at her chest. She froze.

"Who, Quinn? You think *I'm* working for *him*? I'm not...far from it...and I think it's pretty obvious you're not either. Who sent you? I wasn't aware there were any contracts out on him other than mine."

In the excitement of the situation and despite his earlier observations, it just now caught up to Roman that this girl was young, far younger than he had previously thought. "Wait, who did send you? You are way too young for wetwork. What are you, like, fifteen?"

The girl colored slightly, and she snarled, "I'm old enough to rid the world of monsters like you! How old are you, like, eighty?"

Roman grinned and lowered his gun, relaxing. "Now that's just mean, girl. That was uncalled for. "

He glanced around the room as he clicked the safety on. "So we're here for the same reason basically. But yours sounds personal. I don't know what he's done to you to merit such animosity, but I will have to ask for you to reconsider your position. I can get to him and have the job done quietly and quickly, without," he glanced at the sword hilt, "um...bloodshed?"

He slipped the gun into its hiding place under his armpit. He took the opportunity to tap a code on the tattoo on his chest, a stand-down order in case Rosalyn had started an extraction. Where was she, come to think of it? He hadn't heard from her since they got back here. His eyes flitted to the glass bubble he had noticed in the ceiling behind the girl, almost unnoticeable to the untrained eye. Ah, jammers. That made sense.

She hissed and pointed the hilt at him. "No, you just stay out of my way, whoever you are! You don't know what you are mixed up in. I must confront him and take him down...it is my duty. The Order does not allow civilians to interfere..." she caught herself. Roman raised an eyebrow.

"The Order? Never heard of an order. But I'm no civilian, girl, and I know more than you think. I'm one of the best at what I do. I get the job done. And that job is..." he stopped when her gaze shifted behind him. He saw enough in the reflection of her eyes to turn around with his hands raised. Standing in the now open doorway was Aaron Sanders, Sean Quinn's personal assistant and right-hand man. Behind Sanders, towering over him, were two large hefty individuals wearing matching black suits and matching black sunglasses. And pointing matching machine pistols in the general vicinity of the entire room.

Aaron spread his hands, the smile on his face never reaching his hard black eyes. They glittered behind small circular glasses.

"Mr. Stephanos, my how we worried about you. You disappeared with this server," the black eyes took her in and subsequently dismissed her, "when the festivities were just starting to peak. And leaving your beautiful guest unattended...such a faux paux." His voice never changed in modulation or tone.

Roman drudged up a reassuring smile as he subtly shifted his body to put himself in between her and the goons. "Evening Aaron. I'm glad to see you! As you can see, we're just fine, just having a little talk. Perfectly innocent, you don't even need to mention it to her. I was just making sure she wasn't traumatized by my slipup out there. I'll be getting back to Christy now, I know she must be getting antsy without me by her side. And I'm sure this server has to get back to work as well." He moved to step forward, then froze as red dots appeared on his chest.

Aaron shook his head. "Your date is being well taken care of by her many admirers. You needn't worry on her behalf. I would worry about yours. You will be coming with us, Mr. Stephanos. Mr. Quinn wants to speak to you. Wolfgang here will take care of the girl." He gestured to the gorilla to his right, who broke his stony grimace to smirk at Dolores.

"No. Absolutely not. She comes with me. She stays within my sight. Call your goon off." Just like that Roman dropped the Gregori Stephanos persona and the hardened special agent stared holes into the assistant. There was no menace in his voice, just a promise.

Aaron narrowed his eyes at him and opened his mouth, then shrugged. "Suit yourself. As long as you come quietly, Mr. Stephanos." He smiled with his teeth, and moved to one side, waving his hand invitingly.

Roman stepped forward to follow, and dimly heard the girl grunt a warning. He barely felt the sting of the needle in his arm, and as darkness rolled over like a thundercloud his last thought was, twice in less than an hour I've been surprised. I must be getting old. Then black.

He jerked awake as his back slammed into a hard surface. Groggily he opened his eyes in time to see one of the black suits standing back up from cuffing his legs to the chair he was in. He tensed and felt more cuffs on his wrists, probably chained to the arms of the chair. Neatly subdued, no fuss, no muss, he thought bitterly. A rustling to his left turned out to be the girl, eyes closed, being secured in the same way by the suit's twin. The two men, having completed their jobs quickly and efficiently, exited the room without so much as a backward glance and shut the door firmly behind them.

Roman scanned the room quickly, then more slowly with growing concern. It worried him that their surroundings were so mundane. It appeared they were in a luxurious conference room, state of the art, with huge bay windows on one side and a long ebony conference table on the other surrounded by quality ergonomic office chairs (not one of the ones he and the girl were strapped to he noted). The walls were covered in motivational prints, and the table was overlooked by a giant flat-screen monitor. They were near the windows, and though the lights in the room were dim, there was plenty of light from the city itself coming through the windows. Ah, they must be in Quinn's inner sanctum, his personal office suites in his tower downtown. He cast another look at the girl to make sure she was doing okay and found her glaring at him.

He started, then realized immediately why she was upset. He raised his eyebrows incredulously. "Surely you are not blaming our predicament on me?"

"Of course this is your fault! This never would have happened if you had stayed out of my way and let me perform my duty. You are an incompetent and a fool and a ..." her words transitioned to French, and he guessed from the heat in her voice that they were not complimentary. He let her continue as he studied the room and the chairs they were sitting in. She wound down as she saw what he was doing. She looked down at her wrists and yanked at her cuffs to test their slack, then wiggled in the chair, leaning to one side and then the other. He knew exactly what she was doing. He had already surreptitiously done the same.

"Save your energy, they've taken everything we had. All of our gear is over there on the table." He had spotted them earlier. Besides his earpiece and personal effects, he could feel the raw spot on his chest where the electronic tattoo had been ripped off. His gadgets were lying next to what had to be her gear. He studied them with interest.

The empty hilt was there. This was his first real look at it. It was beautiful, exquisitely wrought. It looked like a medieval sword hilt with gold thread woven through the handle and guard. There was no opening for the blade, however. Like it had been designed without a blade. Besides the hilt, there was a long skinny dagger with an ivory hilt, a leather bracer full of throwing spikes, an old small leather-bound book that looked like it had seen better days, and a silver bracelet with small metal charms hanging from it.

"Traveling light I see," he said wryly as he watched her take in their surroundings as well. His only response was another angry glare. That wouldn't do. They needed to cooperate or they were both in trouble. He had rarely been in this situation before, having been captured plenty of times but never with another prisoner beside him, but he knew that there had to be uncomfortably open communication.

"Listen, we need to calm down and think things through. Obviously, Quinn got the drop on both of us, regardless of who's fault it may or may not have been." He pulled at the cuffs on his wrists. "Personally, this feels like he had advance notice about tonight from somewhere. They knew who I was and exactly what tools I had at my disposal. I feel like us taking each other on was a lucky break for them, but considering they already had hypodermics ready, they were ready for us."

He sighed. "But setting all that aside, we need to work together. I know you don't like me, even though you don't even know me But that's not important right now. What is important is that we have to get free and away from here to somewhere safe, then we can argue about who gets to take him out from the luxury of not being tied up in the target's room."

She stopped fidgeting about as she considered his words. Her young face was unaccustomed to concealing her emotions; he watched every thought play out as if she had voiced them out loud. Finally, with visible reluctance, she nodded. "Very well, you make a good point. I will agree to work with you. For now."

He smiled and let out an exaggerated breath. "Good, glad you could see things my way." He grinned wider when she narrowed her eyes. "Okay, okay, let's start by actually introducing ourselves and who we're presenting here. That might help us figure out who gets to do what, and maybe we can connect some dots on how Quinn knew about us. You can come clean, I know you're going by Dolores, but you don't look like a Dolores."

She pursed her lips, then said, "My actual name is Eve. I've been sent by the Order of Tares to eliminate Sean Quinn, at any cost."

Roman filed away the unfamiliar name. "We'll come back to that.My turn. My real name is Roman Capule. I've also been sent to make sure Mr. Quinn meets an unfortunate end tonight. That dart gun over there was intended to be used to ensure Quinn had a heart attack tonight. I'm an operative under contract to the Robinson Estates."

Eve paled visibly and her eyes widened. "Oh no," she whispered.

"Oh yes my dear," interjected an unfamiliar voice. Both heads snapped to the open doorway, where the tuxedo-clad figure of Sean Quinn was standing. He was removing his black leather gloves as the two guards reached in to close the door behind him. It was said that he had an aversion to touching anything, as he was never seen without gloves.

"He is indeed a super secret special agent, a spy, a saboteur, an assassin. That's two zeroes and a seven, correct?" He laughed to himself, obviously amused.

"It took me far too long to figure out who you were, Mr. *Stephanos*. Kudos to you, sir," he tipped an imaginary hat to Roman, who merely watched grimly. "I'm usually pretty good about picking up on your type, but you are as good as your reputation. I've heard so much about the great Roman Capule...I just never expected to meet you face-to-face. I am honored. It's not every day that you merit a visit from the highest paid over-the-hill assassin in the world." Roman grimaced.

Quinn turned to Eve. "You, however, my exotic young filly, are an enigma to me. There doesn't seem to be any information about you. Anywhere. Very unusual. So my question is," he walked over and stood in front of her, still smiling, still playing the inquisitive host, "Who are you?" The smile could not quite conceal the hard steel in his voice.

She just looked up at him, her mouth pressed close, her eyes communicating her response. Without a change in expression, he slapped her across the face with the glove. She rocked back, more from the shock than the force, then growled and tried to leap at him, teeth bared, but the restraints held. Quinn casually reached out and pushed her back in her chair.

"Who. Are. You. I won't say it again. You aren't just a disgruntled subject or a professional like him. This, for example," he reached over and patted the dagger, "should no longer exist. Especially not in the hands of a little girl like you."

Roman saw it before he could stop it. The rage made her throw her shoulders back and look him squarely in the eyes. "I am not an assassin, monster. I am Eve Strauss, of the Order of Tares, and I will be your undoing."

Roman managed to break in, glaring at her to shut her up. "Is all this necessary, Quinn? She's a bystander, collateral damage. This is between me and you. Leave her out of it, she's not a part of it. Uncuff me and we'll settle this man to man..."

"Demon."

It was said flatly, under her breath, dropping like a pin drop into the sudden silence. They barely heard it. Barely. But both immediately froze, one in confusion.

"What," Quinn said, unnerved. He was frowning, a strange expression on his face.

"Demon. I name you, demon. Lesifuges, Bringer of Riches and Shortener of Life. You killed my father, you brought about the downfall of hundreds of innocents, you are corruption in the flesh. I have been sent by the Order of Tares on a holy mission to destroy your kind. You have been marked for death by those who know what you are."

Both men stared at the girl. Roman's jaw had dropped open completely in incredulity. He was starting to wonder about the girl's mental health. Eve seemed a bit on the unbalanced side. Demons? Holy missions?

"Eve...," he started, trying to repair the damage and smooth things over, such as he could. He felt, he knew, that he could still bring this back to a reasonable place where he could talk them out of danger. He was interrupted.

"Interesting. How is that name still remembered in this world?" Quinn mused, amused surprise coloring his words. Quinn, clearly recovered from his initial shock, tapped a thoughtful finger on his chin. "I thought I had managed to destroy all remnants of my title. And the Order of Tares? Seriously? That pathetic little hunting club was broken up decades ago, or so I had heard. Amazing the resilience of you little cockroaches. So what, girl, does that make you a demon hunter?" He laughed cruelly.

Roman was starting to feel like he was losing control of the situation.

"Yes," she hissed at him. "Like my father before me. Murderous monster. Demonic scum."

"Like your father, Strauss you say?" Quinn lifted an eyebrow. "I don't think I've ever met a demon hunter by the name of Strauss."

"Listen, wait, let's start over, neither of you is making sense..."

Both ignored him.

"I took my mother's name, as is proper. My father was the legendary hunter Joseph Henry."

Quinn's eyes lit up. "Yes, that name is known to me! We did tangle a time or two. But you've been misinformed, my little demon hunter. I did not kill him. I did want to. He slipped away before I could get my hands on him. Not before he dismantled my organization in Bogota." He rubbed his chin. "But it seems the distinction of that kill went to another. Shame. I could've made some money from that video."

"Are you two insane?" Roman blurted out. The two turned to stare at him as if he had just appeared. "You're talking about demons and hunters like it's normal? Do you expect me to believe that this is real? How am I supposed to...to..." Roman trailed off as he finally noticed Quinn's grin. It just kept getting bigger and bigger. It started to wrap around his suddenly bald and scaly head. His eyes were burning purple embers. Had Quinn always been tall, so tall he towered over Roman?

More importantly, had Quinn always had a second set of spindly arms, tipped with razor-sharp talons?

Sean Quinn laughed hoarsely as Roman drew back in horror, his eyes wide in shock. "Poor, pathetic little Roman. You are just now realizing that you are in over your head. You never could have hurt me, dog. You have been lucky not to encounter me before, but your luck has run out. You were intended for a far more lucrative outcome." His violet-dripped eyes swiveled to Eve, who was staring at him wide-eyed, but somehow unsurprised. "Don't get cocky, my little huntress. Your presence here was a surprise tonight, but it worked to my advantage. Did you really believe an apprentice child like you could take down a demon lord such as myself when your father couldn't even do it? Even your toys are nothing more than that...playthings in the hands of a little girl pretending to be like her dead daddy; a no-name, pathetic demon-hunting failure from the island."

Eve choked on a squeal of rage and lunged at him again and again as he roared with laughter, throwing herself against the metal links as the chair rocked from the force of her fury.

"Legendary?" he sneered. "You and I wll be the only ones who will ever know the name Joseph Henry, and soon it will be just me."

Then he stopped and leered, his red-slitted eyes roving up and down her body as she struggled fruitlessly.

"You're lucky I'm not one of those demons that takes pleasure in the taking of human females, my little huntress. You'd make a fine specimen." Eve spat at him, and Roman broke out of his paralysis to yank at his own bonds, involuntarily growling. Quinn chuckled viciously and held up a claw.

"No need to fret, cockroaches. My tastes don't run so deviant. But that of others do. Your worth to me is far greater as a profitable prize, my little huntress. Your purity and your heritage will make you a precious commodity to those who value such things. Get comfortable, my very important guests," he said as he fixed his cufflinks, now back in his human guise. "I'll be back with hopefully a better idea of what to do with you. Maybe an auction?" He adjusted his suit and smirked at Roman. "Then we can continue tonight's main event. Before we were so rudely interrupted. Don't worry about any appointments you have to make. I have a feeling we're going to be here for a long while. No no, don't bother getting up, I'll see myself out."

Still chuckling to himself, Quinn walked out of the conference room. The double doors slowly closed behind him. The barest glimpse of the two guards falling in step behind him was the last view they had.

Eve screamed at the door, she cursed in several languages, she rocked back and forth in the chair and beat at the cuffs so much Roman could see her wrists start to suffer. She couldn't, wouldn't hear him. Nothing he said made a dent in the girl's frenzy. He wasn't even sure how much of it was fury, frustration, or fear, but he knew there was quite a bit of all emotion pouring out of her in a torrent that she didn't know how to control.

After quite some time of that, she suddenly collapsed back in her chair, her chest rising and falling heavily, her head turned away from him. The violence had made her hair come loose completely, and the swinging tresses hid her face from him. Thus he was completely floored when he heard her sobbing.

Roman was above all things a professional. He prided himself on having the experience and skill to get through whatever life threw at him. Life had thrown a lot at him his entire life. But as he watched the young girl breaking, he vividly recalled that sharp fear and helplessness he felt when he had first started this game. Plus, he was a sucker for a woman crying. He wasn't made of stone, after all.

"There was a mission, back probably before you were born. It was in South America...I can't say where exactly, still confidential I think. I was still in the service but in special operations by that point. Our unit was being dropped into the jungle to capture some foreign national's cousin. It was supposed to be a fast grab-and-dash mission, no surprises, no curveballs. We took off in a camouflaged cargo plane from a hidden airstrip that had been retrofitted just for this maneuver and were running silent in the dead of night. Everybody suited up. Cargo hatch opens. We go to jump and immediately come under fire, as soon as the last team, my team, launched. It was like they knew exactly where we were, exactly at what time, exactly who to hit. I was only twenty-two at the time, young enough to feel like I could pick up whatever I needed to know along the way but old enough to have known better. I hadn't bothered letting anyone know I didn't know the first thing about HALO jumping, and definitely nothing about aerial evasive maneuvers."

He looked up at the ceiling, reliving that terrifying moment when he had realized he was going to die, feeling again the gut-wrenching fear that had almost overwhelmed him. Dimly he heard her stop crying. "These were trained soldiers, experts in what they were there to do. More than capable of holding off a few rogue commandos or some paid mercenaries. But this...this was more than that, more than what we were ready for." He licked his lips. "The marine tasked to guard me was...shredded...before my eyes. She saw my panic and had acted as soon as the guns started firing, kicking me away from the rest of the team and activating my emergency chute. She died trying to save me. I can still hear the bullets thudding into the bodies around me, the roars of the guns, the men, and women, around me screaming. Screaming orders, screaming directions, screaming in pain. And all I could do was shut my eyes and pray. Pray that I would make it through the gunfire, through the darkness, through the landing. I never felt so helpless in my entire life, and I never have since. I promised myself and whoever I was praying to that I would never again be caught so vulnerable again."

He stopped, too aware. He was looking out the window and searching the night sky, trying to find the moon. He wasn't sure how long they had been left alone. Over an hour, he guessed.

There was a warm silence. He wasn't surprised to hear her hoarse voice. "I am guessing you made it. The Lord works in mysterious ways. Thank you for the reminder that He does answer prayers, even the ones of those who do not believe on Him."

She paused as he looked back at her, She had composed herself, and although her eyes were still puffy they were clear, and no longer looked as maniacal. She pursed her lips and took a deep breath. "I am sorry for blaming you for this. It is obvious you did not know what was happening, what the truth of the situation was. I am sure demons do not come up in your line of work, at least not quite as blatantly.

She hesitated. "And I am sorry about your plight. I didn't realize that you had been sent on a suicide mission."

He was nodding agreeably but started at the last. "Say what?"

She looked away for a moment, and chewed on her lower lip in obvious consternation, then took a deep breath and looked straight into his eyes. "The Robinson Estates. Your employers. They know Sean Quinn is a demon. They knew you would fail your mission and be captured. They sent you here likely as a sacrifice to him. They sent you here to die."

He blinked at her, slowly. "And how did you come to this conclusion? With your supernatural hunter powers?"

She bit her lip and jerked her chin at the table. "The Robinson Estates is mentioned in my father's journal. They serve the demons and monsters as a haven in the world of mankind, a sort of middleman or broker. They are a cabal of vampire lords."

Roman nodded, still reeling but not letting it engulf him again. He wasn't sure how much to trust her. But then again, there was Quinn. He changed the subject so that he could have time to process this new information. "So, if you don't mind me asking, who's your father?"

Eve was silent for a bit, considering. "Joseph Henry was born and raised in Jamaica, in Spanish Town. There...there was an incident involving vampires there, with his first family, and he was left for dead.

He vowed to hunt down those responsible, even if no one believed him about the existence of the creatures. His inquiries eventually revealed to him the presence of a sect of hunters left over from the Spanish Inquisition and traveled to Trier, Germany."

"They were called the Order of Tares, created by Friedrich Spee, a former witch confessor from the Inquisition, and run by Jesuit priests under the guise of a mission. My father started training to become the best hunter in the world, to eliminate what he now understood to be the demon taint among mankind. He met Mother during that time, a direct descendant of Spee and another trainee, an aspiring huntress. Lineage is traced through the mother in the Order, you see. It has something to do with the ability to store the power. My father and mother married soon after graduation and began working in the field as a team. Mother was nine months pregnant when the castle that housed the Order was destroyed. She gave birth to me in the forest outside as they fled the siege. A barghest found them and she held it off while my father took me to safety. That was the last time we ever saw her. He trained me to be a hunter, moving all over Europe and Asia, raising me as best as he could in between his own crusade to avenge his family and the Order and my mother."

She exhaled deeply, looking down at the floor, her expression mournful. "Three years ago he left me with some trusted priests and went after what he believed to be a solid lead on the demon who led the attack on the castle. He sent me a message by bird assuring me that he was close and that he was in the Americas. That was the last time anybody heard from him."

Roman listened to this tale in disbelief. He didn't want to believe this story about secret monster-hunting societies, but he no longer had the luxury of doubt, having been exposed to Quinn's monstrous transformation. As Eve finished, something struck him.

"Quinn said something about being an amateur. You said you were trained since birth, but is this your first time in actual combat, girl?"

Eve blushed. The edges of her mouth curled upwards as she flashed a quick smile that disappeared just as fast. Her eyes darted over to his and then flinched away. "Actually, yes. I trained as best as I could under those priests, who were very good at various forms of combat, and I studied my father's books and personal journals extensively. He had a tremendous knowledge of the inner workings of the demon world, not just acquired from the Order's books, but also from actual experience. He kept his most important information in his journal over there. Those were his personal notes and intelligence that he was able to personally verify and that pertained to his personal quest. That's how I know about the Robinson Estates. He discovered they are heavily involved in the medical and pharmaceutical industries clandestinely. They pull a lot of major strings for their kind. He just didn't know any of the specifics about them, like where their main quarters are based or the human identities of the members."

Roman shook his head. The thought that it was fortunate that the comms were inactive had struck him suddenly. Rosalyn had come to mind, and an ice cube formed in the pit of his stomach that slowly started to burn hot. "I might know quite a bit about all that. I might know much more than they intended me to know." His skin burned as he thought about how he had been used all these years, on missions he had believed to be righteous, and then to be thrown away at the end, without ever knowing the rules of the game. The real game, as it turned out.

Eve shrugged and continued. "The priests refused to let me leave, telling me it was too dangerous, that I was too young and inexperienced, and generally indicating that I would fail because I was a woman. I did not like that. I am just as effective a hunter as my mother was, they were just misogynist priests. And I needed to find my father. I figured I would have a better chance of finding him if I followed in his footsteps along his quest. I snuck out in the middle of the night with my mother's weapons and my father's books. This is all I have. I came straight here to the first entry in my father's journals of known demons and monsters with the most influence. I did not know if Quinn truly was involved in the fall of the Order, but I knew he was an enemy of all mankind, and I might get some information from him."

Eve sighed. "Not that it matters at present. We're trapped, captured like prey by a demon, and you're going to be sacrificed, and I'm going to be made a demon bride."

Roman coughed convincingly to cover up his sudden discomfort. It appeared she was still very innocent about some worldly matters. "Well, actually, not really. I don't think you quite grasped the point of my story. I vowed never to be vulnerable and checked as long as I'm still capable of doing something about it." He held up his freed hands and grinned. "And as long as I'm awake, I can always do something about it."

Eve's jaw dropped. "How in the world...?"

Roman held out the handcuff key he had hidden. "Would you believe magic camp? No time to explain anymore, we have work to do. Quinn's going to be back any second. We have a chance to get the jump on him, but we have to work together to do it, and quickly. I get that you know supernatural weaknesses and such, and have special ways of taking him out...you have to trust I know quite a bit more than you about covert action and ambushes and real-time combat strategy. I am willing to trust you; will you trust me?"

Eve looked at the proffered key for only a second, then looked him square in the eye. "Yes."

Quinn flung the doors open and strode into the room with an easy step, smiling down at what was written on the sheet of paper in his hand. He didn't even bother to look up.

"Good news, my little strumpet. You were the subject of an intense bidding war, but there's been a winner. You'll be pleased to know that..." He stopped abruptly as he sensed the change in the room. In one fluid motion, he dropped the paper and swung an appendage up to block the attack on his left as he expanded. Roman had managed to get close enough with the long skinny dagger with the ivory hilt to strike at his flank but only managed to nick him before he was thrown back by the force of Quinn's counterattack. Even so, Quinn hissed in pain and his lower right arm went to the wound. He jerked it back as if burned.

The dagger is a rare metal believed to have been mined from a meteorite, blessed and anointed by the Jesuits, and is storied to contain a petrified splinter from the True Cross within its core. It grieves their kind and poisons them like acid. Eve's voice rang in Roman's memory.

"What are you playing at, Capule? Are you trying to be a hero now? Do you think you can take me?" he roared. "I caused the collapse of the Roman Empire because I was BORED! You are ants to me, bugs to be used and smashed!" His lower extremities grew sickly green glowing claws, and he launched himself at Roman.

The agent met him head-on. He flipped the dagger into his right gloved hand and thumbed a pad on the palm of his left. The smell of ozone crackled in the room and Quinn growled as the electrical charge traveled down the dagger and shot into his chest. Though it didn't appear to injure him much, he did stop in his tracks and draw a deep breath. He then sneezed, a grotesque sickly bark, and scratched at the spot where the bolt hit him.

Electricity itself doesn't do much to a demon other than reveal their invulnerability to it, but maybe mixed with the holy metal it will at least cause a reaction. However, that's only a theory my father had. Chalk one up for Daddy Joe, Roman thought and skirted around the table away from the still-growing monster.

For his part, Quinn wasn't stupid. He instantly smelled the trap and whirled around. Eve had stepped out from behind the door holding the brace of throwing spikes. He sneered, the expression monstrous on his shifting face.

"Daddy's little huntress, come to redeem your honor? You're as ungainly as a giraffe and twice as ugly. You can't hope to do half as well as your silver fox here has. At least you've sense enough to leave the fighting to the men..." A flash of metallic light and a throwing spike grew out of his left eye. His scream of rage and pain made her flinch back, and he rushed her. She stood her ground and let fly every spike she had with unerring accuracy. The silver shivs sprouted from every part of his body, but Roman saw she would run out before Quinn closed.

"Now!" he shouted, and he threw the dagger at the demon's exposed back. Quick as a cat Quinn spun back around and caught the blade in one claw. A wicked grin spread across his face as he crushed the dagger to pieces, purple ichor still dripping off his chin. His jaw dropped in what could only be described as a howl of victorious laughter.

"YOU STUPID, INSIGNIFICANT..."

His expression changed abruptly to shock as a bluish-glowing sword erupted from his chest, radiant and white-hot.

The sword was forged by Friedreich Spee himself in his last years, in ways that we can no longer understand or duplicate. It is fueled by faithful and righteous anger, and can only be wielded by one pure in faith and spirit and body. My mother used it until she married, and then she kept it to hand down to her child. The blade itself is immaterial, only manifesting when in the presence of those that don't belong to this world, and it is impervious and invisible to all their powers and magicks. It destroys such outsiders on contact. Like demons.

"No," he whispered hoarsely. Eve was braced behind him, holding the hilt with both hands, the sword's glow enveloping her in an angelic halo.

"Yes, my little demon," she spat through gritted teeth. "May the grace of the Lord have mercy on the filth you call a soul." Then his body collapsed to the floor and melted into a purple-green ooze that evaporated into vapor within seconds. All that was left was a large gold coin with a strange symbol on it. Huntress and agent stared at each other over it, chests heaving. He grinned at her. "Not bad for a first assignment, girl." She smiled back in weary triumph.

"Hey Rosalyn, you still there?"

"Roman! Where the blazes have you been? You fell off the grid hours ago! Are you alright? What happened?"

"I'm fine, got a scare when his men walked in on us and dragged me into a shielded backroom, and in the tussle, I think some of my equipment got damaged. I had to take off and lay low. I think I'm in the clear for now. How's Christy?"

"Soon after you disappeared with that waitress she got approached by Aaron Sanders. He asked her some questions about you then disappeared too. He came back after half an hour and basically just took over your date with her. They went home together."

"Not surprised. Listen, I..."

"Where's Quinn, Roman? His limo was spotted leaving the mansion and headed downtown. We lost connection to him once he got to his office."

"No idea. I never got to get close enough. I think he made me. It might've been that other hitter. I lost her when the goons grabbed me. I'm gonna have to do a disappearing act for a bit myself to make sure, maybe come up with another angle to go at him. Let the sponsors know the contract is still valid, but I'll need more time. My rates will adjust accordingly."

A hesitant chuckle. "No problem, Roman. For you anything. Check in as soon as you can." A pregnant pause, then almost too casually, "By the way, did you ever find out what was the deal with that girl?"

Roman closed his eyes. He almost wished he could reach through the phone and choke her. Instead, he kept his voice calm and level, and responded back, slightly confused.

"Not a thing. She denied being there on contract, but before I could find out more we were attacked. She took off during the fight. You get anything on her?"

"Nothing, there is no record on her whatsoever. She was probably just a red herring. I would just forget about her." It spilled out all in a rush, her breathy voice in his ear pitched a little higher than normal. "Keep yourself safe and get back to the Estates, agent."

"Copy that." He hesitated, then said, "I'll get with you later, Rosalyn."

Roman dropped the earpiece to the floor and stomped on it. He then looked up into the expectant green eyes of his new partner.

"Let's get them."

CHAPTER II

The Robinson Estates

Eve stared grimly at the iron gates. "This isn't going to work, Roman."

Roman shot her an irritated look and huffed. "Sure it is, this is foolproof. They don't know anything about what's going on, it's unlikely those guards have any specific orders about me, and they wouldn't be expecting such a brazen attempt at entry even if they did."

Eve Strauss shook her head. "That may be true for any other than the demontainted. But vampires have long lives, with decades or more to plan and prepare, and are known to concoct convoluted schemes, and dey have access to resources not available to the common criminal. Also, those two men there are not human." Her Jamaican accent was strong but her enunciation was clear and concise.

Roman Capule stopped pulling equipment from his bag of tricks and looked again at the two guards lounging designedly outside the giant iron gates to the vast wealthy gated community known to the public as the Robinson Estates.

The two of them were in a Sprinter panel van that had yielded unlocked doors to his delicate touch. On leaving Quinn's complex, they had hiked the seven blocks to one of Roman's safe houses. There they had grabbed what they could of his stashed equipment and weapons. The van had been a lucky break, found in a parking lot behind the strip mall. Roman's own vehicle was still back at the mansion, parked out back as an escape option. In keeping with her low profile, Eve had no car of her own; she had been getting around by taking the bus. He pulled the night vision goggles out of the bag now, held them up to his eyes, and studied the two guards to see if he could see the difference she did.

"They look human enough to me," he grunted. Both men were lean, one taller than the other, and both had kevlar vests underneath blue golf course security jackets. He was willing to bet they were also packing, and more than likely something lethal. Neither looked familiar to him; then again, he had only been here a handful of times, and never at night. It only made sense to have rotating shifts. Plus, as personable and charming as he liked to pretend to be, the faces of guards on security details tended to blur together. They invariably always looked the same.

The mocha-skinned girl was pulling her brown wavy hair back into a ponytail. Her thick lips pursed as her green eyes tried to see over the wall into the compound grounds. She shook her head at him.

"See how they move, almost like they are restraining themselves, like they're ready to leap out and attack, and yet shifting like they uncomfortable in their own skins? They're wearing sunglasses in the middle of the night! Who does that? No, they are beastmen. Creatures of demonic origin, beasts with the minds of men and the bloodlust of animals. Used as servants and footsoldiers for more powerful monsters. They can change their form at will between that of their totem animal and that of a human. The older, more powerful ones can control the change midway, transforming parts of their bodies or even turning into a hybrid creature."

"Huh." The retired special agent, formerly mercenary for hire, currently unemployed assassin zipped up the bag as he took note of her observations. He could see the odd behavior now that she had pointed them out. Although he had only just met the young girl a few hours ago, he fully trusted her knowledge of the supernatural world. A day ago he would've laughed off her delusions about beastmen, demons, and vampires. That was before a demon had tried to kill him earlier that night. Well, the joke was on him. Quinn had been a terrible person anyway. Granted, he was a worst demon, but everybody was better off without him either way.

The tall middle-aged man stroked his clean-shaven face. He could feel the exhaustion threatening to creep in but walled it off like the soldier he used to be. He was no longer dressed in the white tuxedo he had started the night in, but in a snugly dark blue camo hunter's outfit that fit his slim build. The huntress had also discarded her guise;

the server's white shirt she had used to gain entrance to the ball had been left back at the safe house, but she kept on the loose black slacks and grey slip-on sneakers. She wore a black tank top on top that did nothing to hide her runner's build, and he grinned to himself as he saw she was completely unconcerned with how she looked. A true soldier herself. She touched the sword hilt at her side, within easy reach, and finished tying up the bracer of daggers on her left wrist. The small leatherbound journal of her father was tucked in the back of her pants. She was very protective of it, reluctant to even let him look at whatever she had been reading up on.

"Alright, beastmen. That sounds a lot like werewolves to me. Do we have any silver bullets?" He was half joking, half curious.

She flashed a smile at him. "As a matter of fact, I do." She held up her leather bracer full of throwing spikes.

"Hmm. Okay then. Slight change of plans."

"Good evening, gentlemen! How are we tonight?" Roman called out as he sauntered up to the gate. He knew from Eve that their sense of smell was as good as a canine's, so he knew they had already detected him before he had turned the corner. They were standing in front of the gate, silent and watching him, their eyes hidden behind the sunglasses. She had said that the eyes were the only things they had trouble changing, which was probably why they kept the sunglasses on. With their enhanced senses, the tinted glass wouldn't detract from their perception in any significant way.

He plowed on, continuing to walk toward them erratically in the face of their passive hostility. "So I'm a bit lost if you can believe it," he said a little too loudly. "I was trying to visit a good friend who lives in Harmony Hills and got a bit turned around. These places all look the same in the middle of the night. If you could help me out, I'd really preciate it. She's really eager for me to arrive, if you catch my drift." He winked exaggeratedly at the closest one. Still no reaction. "So, uh, yeah, if you could point me in the right direction, I'll be on my wa....oops..."

He had gotten close enough to see the far one flare his nostrils and turn his head to the side, and immediately did his patented stumble into the closest one. The guard snarled at him and pushed him away, and so didn't notice the thud of a throwing spike hitting flesh. He did sense something was wrong, however, and whirled around to see Eve leaping out of the bushes across the street as his partner dropped to the ground soundlessly. The guard immediately lifted a hand to his ear radio as he reached into his jacket with his other one, only to grunt as the spike Roman had hidden up his sleeve slid home between his ribs.

"Nice throw," he said to her as she ran up. As he wiped off the blood from the silver blade, he looked down at the bodies, curious.

She retrieved her spike from the dead body and stood up. Noticing his gaze, she smirked.

"Expecting something?"

He flushed. "Kinda," he murmured. "Aren't they supposed to change back when they die?"

"You Americans watch too many movies, Roman. They simply die. Changing forms is a conscious effort. The pure earth metal in the silver allows us to bypass their lightning-quick regeneration. If you had not struck true, he would have had time to tear you to pieces before he perished."

"Ah. Good to know."

Eve undid the simple latch to the gate, eager to get to the small gatehouse. Only then did she notice the light on the security camera watching them was off. She turned back to him, frowning. He flashed her a smile and held up a small device. "Localized jammer. I activated it as I was walking up. We've been invisible to all prying eyes and ears for the past ten minutes. We'd better hurry though. Somebody is bound to notice there's been static on those screens."

The van was too conspicuously out of place in such an elegant neighborhood; it would draw too much attention. They could approach on foot, but they might be stopped by another patrol. As awful as the idea was, as Eve repeatedly stated, they dragged the guards' bodies into the bushes just inside the gate and stripped them. While out of sight of the road and the cameras, they were still crammed together in the same space. Roman held up the larger guard's pants to compare, and Eve lifted her lip with distaste as she eyed the other set of rumpled clothes. It suddenly struck her what their proximity would entail, and her face paled as she shot Roman a look. He shrugged and held up his hands helplessly in resignation, then very deliberately turned around.

As the two got dressed, with their backs turned to each other, Roman wracked his brain to try to alleviate her palpable discomfort.

"Okay, so tell me some more about this Order of Tares you work for."

There was a grunt behind him, and he felt her shift. "I suppose it is alright for me to reveal more to you since you have saved my life and my freedom multiple times this night."

There was a pause, and then she continued in a more relaxed voice.

"The Order of Tares was founded in 1631 by Father Friedrich Spee, a Jesuit priest. He was a prominent scholar and devout man, who served as confessor to the accused during the Inquisitions in Wurzburg. After ministering to many of the women, he came to feel that most of them had been innocents seduced and corrupted by malevolent forces. His subsequent studies and prayers led him to the discovery of outsiders, supernatural beings not of our world and possibly not of Creation. He named them demons, and founded the Order to hunt them down, judge them by the Word of God, and either destroy them or banish them." She hesitated, then said, "I'm actually not sure which it is. Father's notes aren't clear on what happens when their physical bodies are destroyed here in our world."

Roman had already finished, but he waited until she tapped his shoulder to turn around. Her hair was too much to hide well, but at least the smaller outfit fit her well enough. And the bulletproof vest fit perfectly, which was far more important.

He grinned at her. "So you're really a demon hunter, huh? On a mission from God?"

She narrowed her eyes at him, and he quickly stifled his smile.

"Yes, I am. The Order used to be a powerful battalion on a holy mission, sponsored by the Jesuit priesthood, the hunters blessed by the Lord and armed with His weapons. But after most of the hunters, like Mother, fell during the mysterious attack on their stronghold in Germany two decades ago and the castle was destroyed, there have only been a few left. As far as I know, my father was the last active ordained hunter, and he disappeared three years ago." She squared her shoulders back and lifted her chin. "But he taught me everything he knew, and I have all of his carefully researched notes, and both of my parents' equipment and weapons. More importantly, I have the divine mandate. I will pick up where my father left off, and I will find him and avenge him if need be. I don't know if he is still alive, but I will fulfill his purpose. I may not officially be ordained by the Order, but I am still a hunter trained by the best."

Roman nodded. "I think that I will help you however I can. This has become...uh...personal for me." He smiled as he stuffed his dart gun in the jacket pocket. "It's funny, my brother once told me that I didn't have enough imagination to enjoy fairy tales. But I think this might be the first step towards your goal..if this group is as powerful and connected as you say, someone this powerful will know something of either the castle attack or your father, if we can catch him. We can at least find out more about the connections and individuals that are a part of this, and take them all down."

Eve looked at him, her lips pursed and her eyebrows creased. "What is the ultimate goal tonight? Who are we going after here,

Roman? Is this about purely retributive action, or do you have an idea of our next step?"

"A little. They were very careful not to reveal any details whenever I came around, but there were some things I was able to pick up on."

"Then lead on. Where do we start?"

Roman had been going back and forth on this the whole way over. But there really was no other answer. "To the one who probably has the answers we need. To Rosalyn's house. She'll know how to point us to de la Cruz."

Rosalyn had been his handler with the Robinson Estates since he had started working with them. Supposedly a fellow retired agent, she had been the voice in his head on all of the Estate's missions, though he had never met her face to face. She was a surveillance expert, good at electronics and computers, very smart and experienced. He knew there was no way she didn't know who she was working for.

He had been sent to take out a high-profile target, one who was considered untouchable not just because of who he was but because of the quality of his security. Quinn had disguised himself as a talented and connected pharmaceutical entrepreneur whose lab was developing a much-needed vaccine. But in reality, the drug was ten times more corrosive to the human body than the disease it was created to destroy, and more addictive than fentanyl. At least, that was what he had been told by Rosalyn in confidence, as if she was giving him information he wasn't supposed to know. Instead, it had turned out to be bait, and the trap had been sprung by a fricken demon. If Eve hadn't been there, he would've been offered up as a sacrifice at best.

Someone would pay for making him a patsy. For taking advantage of him and using him. Them trying to kill him without a warning part wasn't terrible...he was used to that, that came with the territory. The betrayal of trust, however tenuous, was what hurt the most. You don't make many friends in this business, and the level of trust is fragile.

Roman had found out where Rosalyn lived completely by accident a few weeks ago. He had come in to meet with Dr. de la Cruz, the money man and his primary contact. They usually met in the spare office at the clubhouse just inside the gates. It was supposedly for convenience, but Roman knew it was to keep him from penetrating too far into the gated community, But this day the good doctor was in the middle of a once-in-a-lifetime golf game and didn't want to stop. Thus, Roman was chauffeured through the neighborhood on the security golf cart, escorted by two alert gate guards, under strict orders to keep him away from anybody's view and avoid streets with people on them.

However, they had turned a corner to find one of the residents bent over the back of a bright green Prius, unloading groceries. One of the guards, the driver, muttered, "Oops, my bad, I didn't know Miss Rosalyn was back in town already" in surprise. The other immediately turned and snarled, "Shut up!" at him, with a furtive glance backward at Roman. For his part, Roman had continued placidly looking at the passing houses without reaction, mentally filing the location and address of the place away. He hadn't been able to see much of the woman anyway, just the back of her and a sense of relative body shape and possibly hair color and style. But recalling the memory now, he felt sure he would be able to pick her out.

That had been over a month ago. That consultation had been for the job prior to the one he had just done, but he recalled with a chill that tonight's had been introduced at that time as well, almost as an afterthought. At the time he had thought nothing of the fact that the guards had talked to de la Cruz before he had been brought to the young doctor. It had been de la Cruz that had arranged this, he realized now with a shock as he connected the dots.

"Who is de la Cruz?" Eve asked as they drove the security cart down the well-lit street. He had already filled her in on Rosalyn earlier as they had left Quinn's building.

"Roosevelt de la Cruz. A bigwig here in the community, some sort of biologist or chemist, a scientist anyway. He was my contact, the guy who gave me the assignments, and the only resident of the Robinson Estates I've ever met in person. From what I've been able to research on my own, he's the grandson of one of the original founders of the group." He paused as he considered that all the way through. "Oh, he is the original founder, isn't he?"

"More than likely. Vampires frequently take on the false identities of their own progeny to throw off suspicion. If he is that connected, he is probably one of the clan leaders. What else do you know of him? Do you know where he is laired? It would be best if we could surprise him, as most vampires are formidable opponents even without advance warning. And if we can cut off one of the heads of this vile serpent, the rest of the group may fall into chaos, chaos that will only serve to help us destroy them all."

Roman grimaced as he made a U-turn. It was difficult enough to navigate his back through the labyrinthine streets of the gated community at the best of times; operating at night from a month-old memory was definitely not the best of times.

"Nope, fraid I don't know enough about him specifically. But I do know someone who would. Oh good, this is it. Here we are." He stopped the cart at the corner where he had first spotted her and glanced down the street. The green Prius was in the driveway. "That house right there is where Rosalyn lives. She should know everything we need to know about where de la Cruz could be and what we would need to take him out. But if she's half as good as I think she is, she'll be difficult to get the drop on. I do have a plan, though."

She looked away from her scrutiny of the house and flashed a half smile at him. "Yes, I have noticed that about you."

Roman blinked. "Did you just make a joke, Eve Strauss?"

"Perhaps. Perhaps I am feeling what I've only read about, the thrill of the hunt. Or more likely the Holy Spirit is rejoicing that I am on the right path. Now, as you enjoy reminding me, you are the battle strategist here. So what is your battle plan, Roman?"

Rosalyn gazed at Roman with fury and not a little bit of fear in her eyes. Well, in one eye. The left eye was swollen shut from a well-placed huntress kick to the face when she had answered the door, followed by a brief struggle in the foyer. Eve didn't seem to take things halfway. He approved of that. Hit hard, hit fast, hit first. He had hesitated too much when the door had opened, his shock at actually seeing her in person and, truthfully, attacking a defenseless woman delaying his reactions.

As she reeled back from that initial attack, Eve grabbed her and dragged her into the house to the kitchen before she had a chance to recover, Roman following with dart gun drawn to watch for anybody else. The house was quiet, and felt empty. Roman had tied her to a high-backed wooden bar stool with duct tape and placed a strip across her mouth. It had all been done within seconds, almost like they had rehearsed it. Roman was impressed that despite her inexperience, Eve seemed to handle herself with speed and efficiency. The target had been taken completely by surprise; the doorway ambush, the initial attack, the rush into the house. It was all the more surprising knowing Rosalyn's supposed training and expertise as he did. Once they had finished tying her up Eve had left to search the rest of the house and make sure there were no surprises.

Roman, in turn, studied his handler. She was older than he had expected, closer to his own age than her voice and mannerisms gave away. She had mousy brown short hair and a sharp angular face. Although she was dressed in an old band t-shirt and baggy jeans, he saw that her figure spoke of a past spent being fit and muscular but of a more recent past fighting suburban housewife syndrome. She would've been attractive in a safe pleasant way if she wasn't working with the villain to kill him.

Roman, too agitated to sit, walked around the kitchen, looking around and noting all the fancy appliances and sleek look. He pulled out a butcher knife from the custom-made knife block, walked back over to her, and tapped her cheek with it. Her eyes followed the blade the whole way.

"Now I'm not some hardcore demon hunter or a divinely appointed supernatural scholar, so I don't know how to test to see if you're really human or not. Based on my own limited experience, though, I have found that demon blood seems to be a different color from a regular person's. Do I need to find that out about you, Rosalyn?" She frantically shook her head.

"Good. Now, I'm going to take the tape off. Not a peep unless it's to answer my questions." He crouched down in front of her and delicately cut the tape off of her mouth.

Rosalyn stretched her jaw, then looked up at him. "Roman, I..."

Quick as a flash Roman drove the knife into the chair right between her legs, the blade rasping against the demin. It slid into the fake wood with a thud. She gasped and rocked back in alarm.

"Not a peep, remember? I was being serious. Deadly serious. So let's get down to business now that we understand each other. Before I ask what I really want to know, let me ask this: is there anybody else in the house we should be concerned with?"

Her jaw clenched and eyes glittering, Rosalyn slowly shook her head again.

"Okay good. That's a good start. Not that I believe you. Eve will flush them out if there is somebody." He hesitated, working the knife out of the wood as he sorted through the rage her presence kept summoning in him.

Finally, he said, "Why? Why me? Why did tonight happen? How long have you known I was being sent to my death? How could you?

You just laughed and joked with me like nothing was happening, pretended to care and commiserate with me, like there wasn't a DEMON ABOUT TO RIP MY THROAT OUT AND YOU WERE JUST GOING TO LET IT HAPPEN! YOU SET ME UP TO DIE!" His voice had been rising and now he was on his feet, screaming into her face, his face red, his hands balled into trembling fists. It took every ounce of willpower left to him not to slam them into her traitorous, backstabbing face.He dropped the knife, not trusting himself with it in his hand anymore.

For her part, Rosalyn had flinched away during the tirade, her eyes closed and tears streaming down her face. She was choking back her sobs. "Please, Roman, I'm sorry, I didn't want to do it, I didn't want it like this, it wasn't my call, I'm so sorry, I didn't want any of this." She kept repeating it over and over again. Roman sat back down on his heels, suddenly exhausted. He listened to her dully for a few minutes, then held up a hand. Gradually her sobs wound down as she regained control of herself. His own rage now spent, he waited patiently, his composure slowly coming back. His mind started to engage back on its professional circuits, finding a way to complete the mission with as little collateral damage as possible. And as much as he hated her, he was starting to suspect that Rosalyn might be part of that collateral damage.

"Alright, alright. It wasn't your call then. Please stop crying. I'll accept that this wasn't all you. At least until I learn otherwise." He ran a hand through his hair. "But that still doesn't change the fact that you were a part of it, that you were complicit in what would have been my murder. And you know..."

"Believe me," she gulped, cutting him off. "It was better than the alternative."

He narrowed his eyes. "What alternative?"

Her eyes flicked to the side.

That was all the warning he got. One second he was kneeling in front of her, and the next he was sailing across the room, the wind knocked out of him and pain radiating out from his chest. His back slammed into the kitchen cabinets on the other side of the island, and he grunted in pained shock. In a daze, he staggered to his feet and focused on what had hit him. His eyes met familiar calm dark eyes, and his blood froze.

"My alternative, Mr. Capule. I proposed to call Mr. White, a specialist close to us, and have you torn to pieces along with anybody and everybody you had ever talked to in your entire life, for one. You should be thanking Rosalyn for sparing you and everybody you've ever loved that option. She was...quite persuasive."

Roosevelt de la Cruz smiled indulgently at Roman, one hand resting on Rosalyn's shoulder, caressing possessively. He was a nondescript man, with carefully cut golden hair and a soft round face adorned with a well-trimmed mustache. He didn't even come up to Roman's shoulder, but his stocky build belied the hidden strength contained within. Incongruously, he had on what Roman would've called jet-set fashion; a stark white polo shirt, loose cream-colored slacks, and green crocs with white crew socks.

The man cocked his head as he loosened Rosalyn's bonds. His eyes never left Roman's. "You are truly an industrious agent, Mr. Capule. You have never failed to impress me. I knew it was a risk to use you, but there are just some jobs that require the expert touch that only someone of your caliber can bring. I'm pleased I was right about that. However, I was so sure I could account for that pesky quick wit of yours, keep you jumping at shadows on your toes long enough to not question. I am very unhappy to find that I was wrong. It doesn't happen often, I assure you. You should feel proud of achieving that."

"De la Cruz," Roman croaked, his head swimming. "Just the guy I've been looking for." He stumbled to an upright position and tried to shake the cobwebs from his head.

"Yes indeed. I have to give you points for linking me with the woman. I thought my pet had hidden her tracks better than that." He shook his head in mock exasperation at her and made a clicking noise with his throat, as if scolding a child, but Roman noticed that her eyes widened in sudden terror.

Roman registered movement out of the corner of his eye. Eve. De la Cruz had his back to the doorway, so he would not have noticed her. Roman's thumb hovered over the button on his shock glove and he side-stepped around the kitchen island, away from the open archway. His eyes flicked toward the butcher block...with any luck, de la Cruz would think that was his objective.

"You tried to kill me, de la Cruz. Without even the good manners of a warning. That would've been the honorable thing to do. Isn't that what your kind used to believe in?" De la Cruz chuckled, not rising to the jibe.

"But worse than that, you used me, manipulated me, tricked me into doing your dirty work, made me think I was doing some good in the world for once in my miserable life, and then turned around and betrayed me. Not even because I was in your way or because you thought I was a threat." He continued pacing closer, passing the rack of knives, around the corner to come face-to-face with his would-be assassin.

"That's why I'm here, why I've come for you. This isn't about some secret organization that's killing the world. It's not about the evil you've probably done throughout your lifetime, if that's what we want to call it It's not even just about you being a monster, an abomination, some freak of nature that sold his soul for a little piece of power. No, you were a monster to me." He leaped forward, holding his hand in front of him.

Three things struck him in that instant. One, there was no thrum of electricity vibrating from his hand. No faint smell of ozone that indicated the shock glove had powered on at all. Two, de la Cruz hadn't reacted the entire time he had come closer, just stood there grinning at him as he casually drew back a hand. And three, Eve was not alone.

His soldier training took over, and he reacted instantly. He changed course in midair and dove down, rolling forward headfirst. He heard/felt the rush of air over him as de la Cruz swiped at him. The vampire's hand never faltered as it struck the island counter and shattered it, spraying Roman with wooden fragments as he rolled back onto his feet. He ended up back behind the island, genuinely frightened, and it was not just from the ease with which de la Cruz was able to move so quickly or casually expend such strength. He grabbed at his key fob and keyed in a scanning sequence. His vision didn't change.

"What's the matter, Mr. Capule? Not notice anything different?" De la Cruz laughed harshly as he ripped away the rest of the tape holding Rosalyn in place. She flinched as his nails tore at her skin. "Oh, I know all about your little gadgets, Mr. Capule. Or should I call you Mr. Bond? That was one of your first weaknesses I was able to account for, your reliance on technology. Your confidence in your sources is entirely far too trusting. You were hit with a targeted EMP blast as soon as you entered my home, keyed to your DNA. See, I can do gadgets too."

"Those words have no meaning for me," Eve's voice broke in from behind. All eyes went to her in surprise. Roman, still blinking, stared at the scene before them.

Eve was standing at the threshold of the dining area and the kitchen, holding one hand behind her back and the other holding the hand of a little boy. The boy couldn't have been more than six or seven, his dirty blonde hair cut military short and still blinking sleep out of his brown eyes. He was still dressed in Elmo pajamas. Holding his other hand was his big sister, a girl of at least thirteen with long blonde hair falling down her back. Her large wide brown eyes were much more clear and alert as she took in the scene before her. She had on a pink and white frilly nightshirt and pajama pants, with white slippers. Roman noted their facial features with shock, and he stole a glance at Rosalyn to see her face pale with a horror that was not for herself.

"Ah, you have found my broodlings. Excellent. This is turning into a family affair. And you must be the Tares huntress everyone is raving about tonight. The underworld has simply been abuzz all about you; your ears must be itching horribly. The Sultan and Sultana will be most disappointed to know you're not wrapped up in a pretty bundle and on your way to enjoying their hospitality."

Eve ignored his comment. "You will release the woman and step back against the wall, demon spawn. Keep your eyes down, I know all the tricks your kind likes to employ. I know that you keep readily available sources near you, like this family. And I know how difficult it would be for you to find another source for the blood that sustains you." She had dropped the boy's hand, and pulled out one of her throwing spikes, and was holding it loosely close to him. The girl put her arms around her brother, but otherwise, the two did not move, looking up at Eve expressionlessly.

Roman, meanwhile, found himself next to the butcher block again. He pulled out a knife from the block and assumed a defensive pose as he inched back toward Eve. The vampire inclined his head slightly in his direction, then returned his gaze to Eve. He laughed.

"And why should I? If you are half as capably taught as you've proven tonight, then you must know how fruitless your efforts are. Unlike our mutual friend from earlier, I am well aware of who you are. I know what you are capable of, and more importantly, what you are not. I know that you cannot hurt those innocent children. There's no point in pretending to use them as bait. And as much as you dislike her and whatever you think she's done, you can't hurt the woman either. No, you are in no position to make threats, huntress. You are actually in a very precarious position right now. But...I want to make this interesting. I want to give you a fighting chance. I will give you the option of walking out of this house, right this second, with no interference from any of my minions who are even now gathering to find out what is happening, with my promise that you'll at least get a sporting chance at escape. If you can make it to the front gate, I will allow you and your partner here to live, for as long as you can keep running. If I hunt you down like the prey that you are before you get there, I will rip out your delectable throat and let you watch me drink your essence."

Roman saw it, the flicker of doubt and fear in her eyes. He knew that de la Cruz had her number. She would not, could not do what was necessary for fieldwork, in wet work. She was not a killer, she was a paladin. She was losing what little control she had of the situation, and instead of coming to his rescue, she had placed herself and the children in danger. He leaped forward to get between her and the pair at the same time as Rosalyn abruptly spun around in the chair and threw the butcher knife at Eve.

In the books, they always talked about how the moment seemed to blur right when the action started, how time slowed down. In his many years of experience as a mercenary and soldier, Roman had found that it was quite the opposite. His senses seemed to heighten, and he was able to perceive much more than normal. It was his body that was usually too slow to react. But in this instance, he really did feel like time had slowed down as he watched de la Cruz move fast, so much faster than should have been possible, moving past him as if he were standing still. He was aware of the shrieks of the children as they disappeared from his sight, his entire focus narrowing down to the spinning knife. It flipped through the air in front of his eyes as he flung a hand out and wrapped it around the hilt. Then he crashed to the floor and skidded to a halt against the far wall. Groggily, he looked up to see what had happened.

The scenario had drastically changed while he had been on the move. In the space of three seconds, de la Cruz had threatened and clashed with Eve, who clutched the glowing sword in front of her protectively. He snarled at her, massive fangs bulging from his mouth. His hands had altered as well, sporting massive misshapen talons now. Rosalyn had taken the distraction her action had afforded her to run to her children to draw them away from the fighting but hadn't made it further than the corner by the side door. There the three huddled and Roman noted that though she was trying to shield them, they did not look afraid. Their expressions reminded him of the glazed looks he would see walking through a homeless shelter, the look of the disconnected, emotion carefully walled off before it spilled out.

De la Cruz lunged at Eve, trying to push her into a mistake, but she held her ground and countered each advance. The two battled back and forth, feints and swings with the sword flashing white with each swipe. Roman tried to get up to go to her aid, but his head rebelled and he fell against the wall again, still stunned.

Then she saw an opening and leaped forward, slashing at his side and connecting with a triumphant yell. The sword flashed bright, and Roman watched with wide eyes, a smile starting to form. But then he stopped as nothing seemed to happen. De la Cruz just stepped back out of reach, grinning. He looked more composed now, less the out-of-control monster. His hands turned back to normal, but his fangs stayed conspicuous as he pretended to wipe at the entry point where the sword should have destroyed him.

"Ah, the fabled sword of Spees himself. His greatest creation. His crowning achievement. His biggest failure. I was wondering where it had disappeared to."

Eve, her mouth open, stared at him, then at the sword. Did it just flicker?

De la Cruz chuckled contemptuously. "My dear, did you really think that tainted blade could hurt me, the author of its creation?"

Eve's head snapped up, her eyes blazing. "This sword was created by Friedrich Spees, to combat evil, using the pureness of faith and the light of the Lord to destroy it, handed down to me by my mother and by her mother all the way from our ancestor, a renowned huntress of your kind and his greatest pupil..."

"Yes, yes, yes, but why did your progenitor have it if Spees made it? Something that powerful, given to a mere woman? No offense, but something like that should have been utilized by a champion, like Excalibur. Why did she merit it? Because she was worthy?" He snorted derisively. "That sap was always interested in the young pretty ones. It was easy to find his weak point. He was less concerned with the habits of demons, and more interested in the habits of the nuns. Know what I mean?" He leered at her and shot Rosalyn a lewd wink. It was a grotesquely intimate act that made her recoil, her face red.

Eve shook with suppressed rage. That and its proximity to the vampire should have given the sword strength, as Roman understood it, but the sword still seemed to continue dimming. He staggered to his feet, the fog in his head starting to fade.

"You make up stories to spare your life, bloodsucker. How would you know these things? You declaim the name of a great man, a man you would not be capable of facing in life."

"A man, dear one," de la Cruz wagged his finger at her. "Subject to the same desires and lusts all of man are subject to. And as for how I know, well, it's because I was there. I'm the one who set Spees up to fall. After all, your foremother was one of my first experiments."

"LIAR!" Eve screamed, leaping forward and blindly slashing with the flickering sword.

De la Cruz dodged out of the way of the wild swings easily, chortling mockingly. "Huntress of great renown indeed! The progenitor of your bloodline was a whore, who rutted with anybody I pointed her at. She couldn't wait to bend over backwards for him, and he took full advantage of that, many times over. Vows of chastity, hah! He might still have been 'teaching' her if she hadn't thrown off her education and gotten saved." He frowned. "I didn't expect to lose my control over her, but by then it didn't matter. She had done her job. She had corrupted the great confessor and introduced the flaw into the sword and into the bloodline. That blade was forged impure, her child was formed impure, with my blood in it and her. You were all meant to be mine along with his head. It's why, when I finally found the whereabouts of the castle several years ago, I ordered the attack. To reclaim my property...both the sword, and her descendants."

Eve, crying and shaking with rage, was making incomprehensible sounds as she swung at him and stumbled. De la Cruz smiled at her. "I'll be honest, I didn't expect to have my property just present itself to me at my front door. But it seems you are still loath to accept the truth. Here, allow me to prove it to you."

He spun around suddenly, catching Roman sneaking up on him, and slammed him back into the island. Roman fell, caught off guard. Quick as a cat the vampire lord turned to meet Eve's downward stroke head-on. And caught the blade in midair. It winked out.

Eve's gasp of horror was overshadowed by the roar of laughter from de la Cruz. He knocked the hilt out of her hand and flexed his razor-sharp talons, ripping into her throat. She fell backward to the ground spurting blood.

De la Cruz advanced on her, chortling. "The Sultan and Sultana may still get their entertainment after all." He smiled down at her. "After I get my fun first, of course." She sobbed as she backed away, holding onto her throat. Blood seeped through her fingers. De la Cruz reached out for her.

"Not today, any day, or ever, de la Cruz."

De la Cruz spun in surprise to find Roman standing before him with the sword hilt clenched in both hands. He was slightly unsteady on his feet, but it was incredible how watching the scene play out in front of him had cleared his mind.

"Really, Roman. Hero cliches? I'm shocked you didn't call me an evildoer while you were at it. And honestly, if you're going to play at being a hero, you really should have a weapon. Haven't you heard? That thing's useless against me." Grinning, he stepped toward him.

"You talk too much," Roman panted, holding the empty hilt and willing it to work. Why wasn't it working? He felt nothing coming from the hilt. There was no light, no weight, no sword. He shook it once.

De la Cruz let out a derisive chuckle. "Oh, this is too much. It only works for the pure, Roman. We both know that ship sailed a long time ago for you." He lunged, talons raised. In desperation Roman swung as if he had a full sword, knowing there was no other way he would be able to face the vampire. Please, he begged. She needs it. We need it. I need it.

The blade narrowly missed de la Cruz's head, flaring white-hot and scorching hair.

Roosevelt de la Cruz jumped back, his eyes wide. He backed away, shaking his head.

"As usual, you never cease to amaze me. I never would have thought it would come alive for you. You truly are a worthy adversary." He glanced over at the helpless Eve, staring at Roman in fascination, and at Rosalyn and her children still huddled in the corner, then looked back at Roman with a smug smile on his face. "Of course, I always knew you would be formidable. I've looked into your family history extensively. You have an impressive bloodline. What your father accomplished...and then there's the untapped potential of your brother. I've long thought about integrating you into my research. I shouldn't be surprised you've proven worthy of challenging me. In fact, you are probably the only one worthy enough to step up beside me."

Roman blinked at this unusual change of conversation. The sword was heavier than he thought, and he was having trouble concentrating. There seemed to be a leaden quality to the air he had not noticed before. And de la Cruz's voice was starting to reverberate in the space between them.

"You are probably the only mortal I would make this offer to, the only one who would be powerful enough and smart enough to accept it. I would offer you immortality, Roman. I would offer you invulnerability. A slight discomfort and you would be better, superior, powerful. I know you have started feeling the effects of your mortality...imagine never feeling that again. Imagine having all of your youthful vigor and strength back again!"

Roman's vision was growing foggy, seeping into his mind. All he could see was de la Cruz's eyes, peering into his mind. He squinted. He had thought the sword was supposed to be weightless, but it was getting heavier by the second. The tip drooped.

"Think of it, Roman! Think of the power you would gain by accepting my gift! We are forever, Roman. We have all the power. That feeling of betrayal you feel? The sense of helplessness you had? Gone. You would call all the shots. You would be in charge, able to do what you want, take what you want. No growing old and losing strength. No retiring from the business. You can come and go however you please."

Roman felt the grogginess in his mind growing. He was having trouble thinking of any reason why de la Cruz's words were not the right decision. The words echoed in his head. The sword sagged some more and almost flickered out. De La Cruz's voice filled the room, filled their ears, drowning out all other thoughts.

"We are the takers, Roman. We are the ones who make the rules. We take whatever we want, whatever we desire. We indulge our secret lusts because we can. The strong get that right. They are *worthy* of that right! This island princess you're traveling with? She's nothing to you. Take her. Make her yours. Show her where her place is, at your feet, beneath you, writhing for your pleasure, submissive to your every whim. She is mere flesh," he drew the word out, "and blood. She is there to serve your every need. She awaits your every command. Look at her, Roman. See how much she wants it. See how much she wants to be your slave."

Roman obediently turned his head and stared at Eve, lying on the floor clutching her throat. Eve had been watching Roman with horror that was rapidly fading into a need to please him, to submit himself to him. Her body flushed with a heat she had never felt. Her father's journal had warned of the vampire's ability to hypnotize with their eyes, but de la Cruz was draining her very sense of self with just his words, his presence. In spite of herself, horribly aware but uncaring, her free hand started to unbutton her shirt. She would offer herself to Roman as soon as he showed the least bit of interest. Hopefully, she would become his favorite pet. She found herself mewling with desire.

Roman, for his part, was feeling things he had long suppressed. He was looking at Eve truly as a woman for the first time that night, as an object of desire. As an empty vessel waiting to be filled. As meat to be used. Not as a partner. Not as a potential protege. Not as a warrior. He struggled to rise above the fog in his mind even as he felt himself reacting to the thoughts of her as his slave, of all women as his slaves.

"She can be yours, Roman. She's the price of admission. Show us you want the power, Roman. You can even have my breeder in the corner too if you'd like. She's outlived her usefulness to me but she is quite experienced. You'll like her."

The whimper that arose from the corner was mixed with bitter sobs as Rosalyn fought herself to keep from ripping off her own clothes. The girl turned the boy's head away resignedly, neither still not reacting.

Not an object of desire. Not a woman to bend to his will. Not meat. Not a slave. Roman saw in his mind's eye the image of a younger version of himself smiling at a pretty woman in BDUs. He saw the purposeful stride of an ebony huntress striding through the crowd, holding back a sword. He struggled and felt himself failing, and the sword faded away, leaving an empty hilt.

De la Cruz's eyes shifted at Rosalyn's exertions, then dropped. "Or maybe I misjudged your tastes. Your secret desires. Would you prefer the little one? That would still work for me, the bloodlines are compatible and the union would be magnificent. As long as you don't leave a permanent mark on her."

Monster. The word blazed whitehot in his mind, bringing with it a ray of light that streamed out of the vampire's smog.

De la Cruz gasped and fell back to one knee, bleeding from the slash that had appeared across his chest. Roman staggered back as well, his eyes nearly blinded from the light. His head was exploding with pain, but it was a good pain, a cleansing fire that swept through his mind and cleared the fog and the vampire's voice away. He gritted his teeth as he tried to concentrate on the vampire, but the slice he had made had taken all of his strength. He went to take a step toward the fallen vampire lord, but went down to one knee instead, still holding the sword before him.

De la Cruz grimaced as his body convulsed with pain, but he still barked a sharp laugh. "I was wrong about you. Pathetic idiot. When I feast on your whore and get my strength back I'll end you slowly. You're too weak to wield the sword properly, fool. This wound is nothing compared to..." he trailed off.

A bloody hand had plucked the white-hot sword out of Roman's hands.

"I'm not," Eve snarled gravelly, and swung the sword in a wide arc. De la Cruz's head, locked in a gruesome smile, rolled to a stop in front of Rosalyn. She was crying freely now, clutching at her children. They simply stared, expressionless. With a deliberateness that bordered on indifference, the girl reached out and gently closed his eyes.

"We have to get out of here now."

Rosalyn broke the uncomfortable silence. She got up, coaxing the children on their feet as well. Her face, though still tear-streaked and puffy, was calm but determined.

Eve was on the floor, leaning reluctantly against the counter as Roman hurriedly tied a ripped-up kitchen towel around her neck.

Though the carotid artery hadn't been sliced, she was still bleeding, and he feared there might be damage to her vocal cords. He was still dazed himself, and his body ached all over. He didn't know if it was just that he was too old, or that he had taken more of a beating than he thought.

Eve tried to snort and failed. "Why?" she rasped weakly. "This place is as good as any other. And why should we listen to the monster's pet?" She spat the last out, and glared at the woman, ignoring Rosalyn's flinch.

Rosalyn shook her head, then met her gaze steadfastly. "Because now that he's dead, several events have been set into motion. First, I'm finally freed from my compulsion to serve him. My duty is now to my kids, and saving them, and to make up for my actions to the two of you. But the more relevant reason is the medical device he had implanted inside of his heart that alerts whoever's on the other end that his heart has stopped. That would be the other two heads of the Ro'benson Cabal, who will most certainly send a team to find out if he truly is dead and to clean up the mess left."

Roman clenched his jaw as he finished tending to Eve's neck. It was more difficult to do without touching her skin, but his head seemed to pound more whenever he dwelled too long on her as a person instead of her as a teammate. "Fine. Seems like it makes sense. We'll believe you for now. Do you have an escape contingency?" He disliked trusting her, but he knew that she was a professional when it came to mission planning. He would sort all this out when they were out of danger.

"Actually, yes. I've contacted an extraction team that they don't know about," she held up a small key fob similar to his, but with only a single button on it, "but we need to hurry downstairs to meet up with them. There's a secret passage in the wine cellar. It's been...a course of action a long time in the making."

Eve tried to stand and almost fell. She was pale from blood loss. He wrapped an arm around her waist to steady her. She tensed immediately, and he knew she was also still dealing with the aftereffects of the vampire's influence. As was he. He looked pointedly away from her and forced his body to relax. "Lead the way. Keep your hands where I can see them. I still don't trust murderers and traitors." He tried not to look directly at any of the women, instead scanning the room around them and noting with dismay the many hidden cameras he missed the first time.

She held the children's hands and started down a hallway ahead of them. They followed her as she opened a closet door to reveal a narrow staircase descending to darkness. As she made her way down, the children immediately behind her, she flicked a light switch as she passed it.

They emerged at the bottom into a wine cellar. She immediately went to an ornate wine shelf opposite them, pulled a bottle out of a rack, and placed it in another rack. There was a click and then the whole section of wall swung open to reveal a circular stone stairwell leading down into gloom. Here, she turned no light on.

As they followed her down into the darkness, the humidity level rose and the sound of water splashing echoed up the steps. When they reached the bottom Rosalyn stopped, put a finger to her lips, and drew back into the shadow, showing for the first time that night her training as a special ops agent. She came back into view almost immediately to lead them out into a large sewer tunnel, beside an actively running underground river. Although the dank and musty air held a hint of the smells that were surely wafting, the stench seemed to be kept at bay by the large flickering torches that were held in sconces in the walls beside the stairwell opening and directly across the way in the opposite wall. This was a preplanned launching site, with a small floating deck tied off immediately before the opening.

By the time they had reached the wine cellar, Roman had started carrying Eve, who was slipping in and out of consciousness, and had almost fallen flat on her face when her legs gave out under her. He gritted his teeth, mentally, and let go of the aberrant thoughts he had experienced from de la Cruz's hypnosis. That's not who I am, he thought. I'm not that person, and I never will be, Father.

"Hey," he prodded her once they stopped at the bottom of the stairs. "Stay awake!" He felt the adrenaline rush from the events of the night abruptly leave him, and he sagged against the wall to one side as he set her down on the ground, arms shaking. He knew she must be feeling even worse. "Say something! Eve!"

"Nothing to say. So tired. Are we home yet?" she murmured.

"Not yet. We're getting there. Stay focused. Concentrate on reciting the alphabet backward, say a verse, do something. You have to stay awake." He felt her pulse in her wrist and worried at how slow it was. He just knew basic first aid, but even if he had been a trained medic he couldn't replace the blood she had lost nor the energy that using the sword might have taken.

Rosalyn, meanwhile, had taken the kids off to the other side and stood against the wall. She stared intently upstream, clearly expecting someone, and clearly avoiding looking at either of them or talking to them.

Silence dropped over them, only interrupted by the gentle splashing of the water. Eve whispered to herself something. All he could hear was something that sounded like *som*; then she whispered out loud. He had to bend close to hear it. "Tell me something. How did you throw off the compulsion? How did you trigger the sword?"

She asked like she expected an answer. Strangely enough, Roman thought he knew it.

"I once knew a girl. Back when I was much younger, when I thought I ruled the world. In my early twenties. She was beautiful, smart, sassy, capable, strong. She had a dry wit that cut you even as you laughed. She knew how to put me in my place, but did it in such a way that it just made me fall for her even more. Stacy Varga. She was short, petite, just a little thing, and could have kicked my butt without breaking a sweat. Well trained. We weren't supposed to be involved with each other. We worked together, we went on missions together, and that sort of thing is highly frowned upon. But we couldn't help falling in love." He paused at that, astonished that he had admitted that out loud to this slip of a girl. His eyes had glazed over as he remembered. Her mocking half smile, the studious look on her face when she was analyzing something, her constant hunt for excitement and adventure.

Eve, meanwhile, studied his face with no hint of the discomfort of earlier, and her eyes widened with sudden insight. "The marine?"

Roman started at her words, then nodded slowly. "It was going to be our last mission together, as just co-workers. I had the ring in my pocket even as we jumped. I was going to do it after we successfully completed the mission. She didn't know. She had been assigned to protect me. For eight, wonderful months. We just clicked." He closed his eyes, seeing it again in excruciating detail. "She had a bad feeling about the mission. From the beginning. She said she didn't trust the asset. She never really explained why, but she was always uncomfortable about him. That night, she insisted on going first. Again, to protect me."

He opened his eyes, his vision blurry, and stared into the dirty water rushing past them. "I watched her die, right in front of my eyes, cut into by gunfire even as she was pulling out her gun to return fire. I saw the look in her eyes as the life left them, as she looked at me that one last time. I know that she wasn't begging me to save her, but that's what I saw. Because I knew then, just as I know now. It was supposed to be me. I was supposed to have gone first. And as her last action was to kick me away, I prayed I wouldn't be next. I could only think of my own skin. I mourned her afterward, and will always, but in that second I was confronted with my worst self, my deepest flaw, and it was ugly."

He looked at Eve. "I think that's why I was able to resist de la Cruz. I've already been exposed to the worst of me, I've been scoured deep down, made to atone for my own inadequacies, I have experienced the best a woman can be for a man, and I threw it away, if only emotionally, if only momentarily. My dad...he would've gotten along with de la Cruz, I think. Their thinking was very similar, seeing people for whatever they could get out of them But I can't see people, especially females, the way his kind does. I couldn't, and still be able to honor her memory. It's what keeps me going." He paused. "Plus, you said that the sword works on purity, right? Maybe that also means purity of focus and purpose, because that I do have in spades. Especially right at that moment. Because I was going to kill him. Even if I had to club him to death with an empty sword hilt."

Eve looked away, her face dark. "You have proven yourself more worthy than I. I could not resist the unnatural compulsion. I wanted what he was saying...and then what he said about my ancestor...he corrupted her and her line and then he degraded me and would have..." she choked to a halt and grimaced in pain as the tears flowed freely down her cheeks. She shifted uncomfortably in his arms, and he felt her pulling away.

Roman shook his head, but couldn't say anything. He didn't know what he could say. He looked up sluggishly and found the boy watching him intently. The girl was huddled next to her mother, staring at Eve with an unfathomable expression on her face. Roman felt a twinge of uneasiness looking at them. He glanced over at Rosalyn, who was still watching the tunnel and pretending unsuccessfully to not be listening.

"Okay, so as long as we have a bit of time, what's your story, Rosalyn, if that's really your name? Are you or are you not working for these monsters? How did you come to be living with him?" He hesitated as he felt the next words come to mind, then plunged on. "Were you and he really...umm...?"

Rosalyn glared at him, her face flushed. "Smooth, Roman. Real smooth. Yes, I was his plaything. Is that what you wanted to hear? Are you happy? I couldn't control myself around him. I did anything he told me to and anything he ordered me to. For years. Decades. For longer than I can remember. I had to. It's how I was bred."

Roman frowned at her. "What?"

Rosalyn sighed, the exhaustion in her face evident. She reached out and hugged the boy closer to her. He clutched her harder in turn.

"I, and my family and by extension my children, are the products of one of de la Cruz's many breeding programs. Back in the Dark Ages before he was cursed, he was some sort of alchemist, bordering on genius. After he turned, he lost what little humanity he had left and started doing some really horrible experiments. Centuries before they discovered genetics, he figured out that bloodlines were the key to the future, whether humans or...other. He felt he could create the perfect slave for any situation with selective breeding and mingling his own blood with ours at the genetic level. You know, because he was so much more superior to us. He has been...pruning...bloodlines, of hundreds of families across the globe for centuries. Secretly arranging marriages, keeping records of births, removing less-than-desirable traits. Most people don't even know he exists...existed."

She reached up and massaged her temples. Roman could easily read the exhaustion in her body. "That's really how he knows about you and your family Roman. That's the reason you were hired. That you were good at your job was icing on the cake and a great excuse to get you close. His plan all along was to draw you into accepting the curse and bringing you to bear. To use you to continue to breed the perfect soldier. Your bloodline was desirable." She made a face. "I don't think he was actually going to use his powers to entice you the way he did upstairs, though. I think he was just going to put you in a coma and use your body as stock."

Roman suppressed a shudder. This was way more far-reaching than he had originally thought. "Wait, isn't...wasn't he a vampire though? I thought they were just about sucking blood and living forever, not, you know, bloodlines. Plus, I met with him outside during the day, the same day I spotted you. I thought sunlight killed them."

"The curse creates a mortis change in the victim, causing internal deterioration but also dramatically slowing down and arresting some vitals which varies from person to person. They're not immortal, they're just extremely long-lived. And the daylight thing is sort of true, but he found a way around it.

De la Cruz was able to create a serum to ensure that his...seed...was still viable. He took full advantage of it, indulging his horrific theories and perversions in the name of science. He believed that his tainted blood was the key to creating stable and powerful mutations. He used his own serums on himself, as well as his experiments. One of them allowed him limited tolerance to UV radiation."

Roslayn hunched her shoulders and laid her head down on the boy's head, shutting her eyes tight. Then she looked up at Roman, the first time she had met his eyes since the battle upstairs. Her brown eyes were brimming with angry, contemptuous tears. "My grandmother, my mother, and I are all directly related to him. We were his most profitable experiments, as well as the targets of his depraved lusts. He was my father, my grandfather, and if I had proved worthy he would have been my sire as well." She said this in a resigned way as if the reality of the horror of her words no longer bothered her. She looked down at the children and wiped her eyes. "These are his children, Christian and Andrea. They are the light of my life and my only reason for living. I did everything I could to protect them from him. But he didn't consider them as his children, he saw them as his experiment's latest results, to be used. Just like the women in my family. Just like me. And he made sure they always knew what their purpose in life was going to be from an early age, where they stood with him. Part of the indoctrination process," she spat bitterly.

Roman glanced down at the girl and found her staring at him. This close, he could see that although her face was a carefully crafted blank mask, her eyes communicated the hopeless despair deep inside, the desperation. He couldn't help but stare back, his face aghast. "Was he really offering her to me?" he whispered hoarsely.

"It wouldn't be the first time," Rosalyn said sadly and reached out to touch the girl's, Andrea's, cheek. She looked up at her mother. "He used that threat many times. It amused him how upset it made me. Thank God it never happened. But it was only going to be a matter of time."

The echoing sounds of a motor briefly drew everyone's attention away. "Who's coming?" Roman asked.

Rosalyn hesitated. Roman was instantly on guard. "Is that a secret, too?" he said, harsher than he intended.

"No, not like that. It's just hard to explain the Black Lotus. I could say they're a group that specializes in dealing with strange situations. A gang of misfits that I only recently made the acquaintance of. I'm pretty sure the Cabal doesn't know about the Black Lotus. They'll help us get to safety, without incident or fear of discovery. They can be trusted."

"Unlike others," muttered Eve. Roman simply nodded. He looked down at Eve to find her eyes closed. He checked her pulse again, just to be on the safe side. Her heartbeat was a little stronger. He raised his head to glare at Rosalyn again. He was starting to regain his cognitive poise, and something else had occurred to him.

"Who is chasing us, Rosalyn? You had mentioned two other leaders? Are they vampires too?"

Rosalyn shrugged wearily. "I'm not exactly sure. I wasn't trusted enough to be let in on the other two branches of the Cabal's inner workings. I know that the senior partner is named Lydia O'Dell. She has been around a lot longer than either of the other two. But if she's not a vampire lord, she's got to be a demon. She's very powerful and very scary. She keeps strange company, and she's the only one without a house on the Estate grounds. She's actually the one more likely to respond personally to this, since both of them deferred to her. But Thomas King is pretty scary himself. He's the third leader, the operations manager, so to speak. He's usually out of the country taking care of Cabal business, but he's here now overseeing a merger with another company."

Roman could feel his heart stop, and lifted his head sharply. "King. Thomas King? Would that be Thomas Alexander King?"

Rosalyn started. She frowned worriedly at him. "Uh, yes…"

"What does he look like?" Roman asked urgently.

"He looks young, like about your girlfriend's age, but he's supposedly as old as de la Cruz was. He's got dark red hair and thick black eyebrows and…Roman, are you alright?"

Roman's head lolled back and hit the wall behind him. He let out a breath. Then took another long deep breath and slowly let it out. His heart was pumping hard now, and he felt the rage coming back again. Rosalyn glanced over to watch the boat pulling up, then turned back and frowned at the expression on his face. "What's wrong?"

"Thomas Alexander King was the name of the asset on that mission, the only other survivor besides me, the one when Stacy died. He's the one who betrayed us."

CHAPTER III

Dallas, TX

The third time the knocking sounded at the door, it was far more insistent and impatient than the previous attempts. Roman checked the peephole to make sure it was who he thought it was and grinned. He patted down his shirt and waited a few more seconds. He could practically feel the man's impatience through the wood. Then he reached up to undo the locks on the door, slowly, and pulled it open.

"Detective Rogers! How surprising to see you out and about at this hour! Don't you people usually have urgent business at the coffee shop right about now?"

The craggy foreboding visage frowned at him. "Mr. Capule. I was beginning to think I was mistaken about you being an early riser." The huge man in the trenchcoat seemed to ignore Roman's opening comment. Instead, his eyes flicked to the open hallway behind Roman.

Roman started to smile even wider at first. For weeks they had played this game, and it seemed only he was enjoying it or even participating.

When he saw where the detective was looking, however, he realized he might have made a strategic mistake.

"So what can I help you with this morning that can't be discussed down at the station," he said smoothly stepping out into the hallway and closing the door behind him, but he knew it was already too late. Although his guests were far too savvy to reveal themselves, they had funny ideas about entering someone's home. And Roman had not thought twice about the pile of shoes, some of them women's, stacked neatly next to the door.

Stan Rogers' face was still expressionless, but Roman thought he could detect the subtle *gotcha* in his eyes.

"Just a few more questions, Mr. Capule. Some new information has come up, and our latest witness seems to have changed his testimony, again, and can no longer be relied upon. Do you have a moment?" The detective's tone made it clear that he didn't care if he did or not.

Roman looked pointedly at his watch, his face no longer amused. For two months the police had been investigating the disappearance and presumed murder of entrepreneurial tech genius Sean Quinn, and he and Eve were still at the top of the list of possible suspects, due to the very public display the two of them had made at the gala, and their very noticeable absence afterward. Roman knew that the only real reason for that was pressure being applied from what remained of the Robinson Estates. The fact that the head detective of the homicide division was the primary on the case was just further proof of that. There had been some notes in Joseph's journal specifically about Detective Stan Rogers.

"I suppose, Detective, although I must really get back to my guests." No point in disguising that now. The policeman's appearance now was no coincidence. Either he had been staking the apartment out, or he had followed one of the group here. Neither option was appetizing.

Rogers had already taken out his notebook and was writing in it.

"Guests, Mr. Capule? That's unusual for you. Actually, the question I have is really for Ms. Strauss, if she's available to speak."

Roman smiled grimly. Of course it was. "Her injuries were quite extensive, as you probably remember from my earlier cross-examinations detective. She's still on bed rest, per instructions from her nurse. Plus, she's on some powerful medications. She's currently sleeping."

The tall man nodded as if he had expected that answer. He hadn't stopped writing.

"Then I'll ask you to relay the question to her and communicate it back to me as soon as you can. We are impatient to close this case up and we still need her to answer one last matter of contention. I'm sure I can count on your integrity on this, right?" The eyes flicked up at Roman, then jumped back down to his notebook. Roman wasn't fooled. He was smiling amicably, but his jaw practically ached from keeping his face loose. He didn't bother answering.

"Getting back to the night in question, we were given the perception from multiple witnesses that you and Ms. Strauss had left together with the individual in question, but you continue to assert, and Ms. Strauss would back you up on this, that there was no contact between the three of you, that is correct?" His eyes flung back up.

"That's correct."

"Despite eyewitness reports that you escorted the young lady out of the hall, and then the next time you are both accounted for she has been on convalescent care in your residence for the past two months?"

"What can I say, I'm just an altruistic kinda guy, especially for beautiful young women. She had nowhere to crash."

"And no record of the assault on her, or descriptions of her assailants?"

"She's not said anything to me, and I don't ask uncomfortable questions."

"I see." Scribble scribble went the pen. "Because my office has been made aware of a message from a foreign dignitary to the email account of Sean Quinn asking to the whereabouts of Eve Strauss. This dignitary seemed to be financially linked to Quinn and his company. It seems this message speaks to a prior arrangement with the young lady."

The Sultan and Sultana. He had completely forgotten about that loose end.

"I'm sorry, but what was the question?"

Rogers looked up steadily into Roman's eyes.

"What is Eve Strauss's connection to this foreign dignitary, and what was this prior arrangement? Did it have anything to do with why Sean Quinn has been missing under violent and mysterious circumstances?"

"Sorry detective. That doesn't ring any bells. I personally don't have any idea about that, but I'll be sure to ask her when she wakes up. I'll make sure to let you know what she says right away."

Rogers' eyes bored into his, unwavering. Roman kept his face passive but briefly wondered if he had lapsed momentarily. Rogers nodded and started writing again, satisfied.

"See that you do, Mr. Capule. I'll be expecting your call. Make sure to keep yourself and Ms. Strauss available for any further information inquiries." He snapped shut his notebook and then leaned forward. "Rest assured, Mr. Capule. I will solve this case. I don't know what the story is here, but I will find out the truth, and I will put the lawbreakers behind bars, whoever they turn out to be." He stared at Roman for a few moments more, then spun on a heel and strode down the hallway.

Roman watched for a moment, sorely tempted to say something snappy at the officer's retreating back. He held off, however, knowing that now was not the time to risk any more exposure.

When the dark-suited man turned the corner out of sight, he relaxed slightly and slipped back inside. He closed the door and double-checked the biometric lock. As he turned to walk down the hallway to the living room, he nodded to the two hulking figures who had positioned themselves next to the doorway. The twins, massive and ugly as sin, Roman had mentally dubbed Frank and Stein. He hadn't really paid attention to their real names, that was on him. The closer one smirked at him as if he could read his thoughts. He flashed Frank (or Stein) a brief thumbs-up as he walked by.

He walked into the crowded living room. Now that the threat of discovery was gone, the occupants relaxed. They started to talk and move around again. Pervading his personal space and filling up all that the small living room could hold, the Black Lotus looked at him expectantly.

Sitting in the only armchair, scowling, was Brock, the leader of this band. Roman had been dealing with the very stocky man for weeks now and still wasn't sure about him other than the very short man's thickly muscled body hid an incredibly sharp mind. He had a thick grey beard that he kept well groomed but was completely bald otherwise, and deep-set black eyes that took in everything but gave nothing back. He was brusque and direct to the point, but his people hopped to attention whenever he spoke with the kind of respect Roman had rarely seen for an officer. Roman had never seen him wear anything other than blue denim overalls with a grimy white t-shirt, a loaded brown leather toolbelt, and thick hobnailed boots.

Rosalyn and Eve were sitting on the couch with Mary, the gang's healer. She was a perky Korean goth girl with a round friendly face who loved to smile and chat. Every time Roman saw her she was always dressed in some variation of black scrubs with smiling skulls. Roman wasn't sure if she was a real nurse or not, but there wasn't a doubt that her presence was helping Eve to recover faster. Today, she was sitting on one end of the couch with Eve beside her so that she could support her. Eve, for her part, was dressed in some baggy pajamas that he had found at the corner drugstore and looked much better than she had for the past few weeks. She was still having trouble speaking louder than a whisper, and whatever venom the vampire had pumped into her had not finished running its course through her body, but the scar on her neck had closed and was mostly healed. Rosalyn, right next to her, had been leaning forward ready to get up, still bleary-eyed from a late night with her kids, but her eyes watching him as he approached, darting away when he looked directly at her. Two months had not diminished the shame she felt around the two of them. For their part, Eve still did not trust her at all, but Roman had come to realize that there wasn't much point in continuing to hold a grudge.

Terra and Hunter, two newer additions to today's meeting, were standing by the patio doors, peeking out into the courtyard. The third man, a lean rangy man in all denim, was leaning against the wall near them. He was a mystery to him.

"Trouble?" Rosalyn asked, anxiously picking at her pants leg. Brock glowered at her.

Roman shook his head, briefly annoyed with himself that his annoyance was obvious. "Just a couple of loose ends I forgot to deal with. But it won't be a problem." Shouldn't be a problem, he amended to himself. "It can wait to be taken care of later." He gave Eve an apologetic look. "We might have to go talk to the good detective when this is all done."

Brock's scowl deepened. "Ye should be wary of that detective, lad. He is a hound to be feared once given a quarry. We have run afoul of him in the past."

"Be that as it may," Roman said dismissively as he nodded to one of the other visitors. "We have work to do, and little enough to do it. I'll handle Detective Rogers in my own time in my own way."

Brock shook his head doubtfully as the indicated man bounced forward excitedly. Franklin was the techie of the group, enamored of all gadgets and tech, and a genius with electronics. His gangly body was bent over nearly double as he hoisted a small black box that looked like an old record player mated with a slide projector, and neither had enjoyed it. It did not look as heavy as he was making it out to seem, but then again the man's scrawny arms didn't look like they could have lifted a shoebox. He sat down cross-legged behind the entertainment center that had been pulled away from the wall and busied himself connecting the mass of unidentifiable wires to the large LCD TV. Roman grinned at the young man, then turned back to Brock.

"Okay, so what's with this emergency meeting? You know the three of us need to be laying low right now. I'm assuming you got some news on King?"

Brock grunted and stroked his beard. He looked pointedly at Rosalyn, who rose to her feet and walked over to stand next to the entertainment center. Meanwhile, Franklin had pulled the TV stand off and laid the screen down flat on the coffee table in the middle of the room.

"We have been keeping tabs on the movements of the agents from the Estates for the past few weeks, and we had a breakthrough earlier this week. We think we now know where King is, and more importantly, we think we have a good idea what he's u-p to."

Everybody leaned forward expectantly. Roman backed up to the wall and leaned against it, almost opposite the denim newcomer and unconsciously mirroring his stance.

"First, a little background. Most of you know some of this, but this team doesn't have all the up-to-date information. I've worked for the Robinson Estates for most of my life under one of the founders, Roosevelt de la Cruz." An abrupt coughing fit from Eve erupted at that moment coincidentally, and Rosalyn's cheeks reddened slightly as she shot Eve a glance. Roman frowned. The strain between the two might be worse than he had figured.

"In all that time, I was privy to a lot of the Cabal's secrets. And even as well placed as I was, I don't have the first clue about the other two founders, Thomas Alexander King or Lydia O'Dell...who they really are, what their past was, or even what they were. They were able to stay hidden in the shadows. They managed different departments than de la Cruz did, and the three kept separate books and personnel. They rarely if ever allowed their people to interact. Now, as we all know, Lydia has completely disappeared since the night de la Cruz was...removed..., but it seems she has taken control of and is still running the remnants of the Robinson Estates solely from wherever she is hiding. We are pretty sure she is still in the country, however. Brock's forces have been harassing them from the shadows, and there have been other forces at play, probably shadow partners and high-placed associates who are taking the opportunity to make their own power plays. It is looking like Lydia is not going to be able to hold onto her power base much longer, so that's been the only good news up until now.

"All of our inquiries dead-ended on King. He fled the country that night, almost immediately when it happened, and hasn't turned up since. He just abandoned all of his assets and accounts. We think he may have had some secret accounts set up somewhere overseas. There has been no trace of him. Until last night. Franklin, are you ready?"

The lean tech leaned out from behind the shelves and gave her a grinning thumbs-up. He flipped a switch on the device in front of him, and lights started to flash on the console. Rosalyn motioned to one of the men in the back, who turned off the overhead lights. The screen flickered to life to reveal a 3D holographic display forming over the television screen. There was a collective murmur as the group watched, fascinated, and everybody drew in closer. Even Brock's eyes raised up in surprise.

The projection was of a satellite picture rendered in exquisite detail, overlooking the earth. Franklin's fingers were busily manipulating tiny levers and dials on the box's side, his tongue sticking out of the side of his mouth as he concentrated on the image. It was so life-like that Roman almost felt like he was free-falling...a sensation that intensified when the image started zooming in to a location. Even as the zoom sped up, the image sharpened and clarified in detail. Many recognized most of the landscape and features that appeared then disappeared offscreen. Roman gave a start as he recognized the location.

"This is the Al-Masalla obelisk of the Temple of Ra-Atum, in Al-Masalla, Cairo. It used to be the religious center of the ancient city of Heliopolis, during the Old Kingdom. We have long suspected that it was a possible source of power, and now agents close to the Black Lotus have found that the pillar itself is the doorway to a pocket dimension, which is where King has been hiding for the past few weeks. It's a sure bet that as well hidden and powerful as it is, it's his base of operations, and he has been working on something big, because there we have monitored several huge energy spikes radiating out from there."

The holographic display rotated around the obelisk as Rosalyn talked, showing the plaza from all sides. Roman, his arms crossed, grunted.

"I still don't get it. Why here? Why Egypt? I can't imagine how much of a good foundation he could have there, and I know there's not enough infrastructure to recover what he's lost."

Rosalyn glanced nervously at Brock. The team leader stroked his beard thoughtfully and regarded Roman.

"It's because King wasn't just a lawyer or monster. Thomas Alexander King was and is the first pharaoh of Egypt, Ra-Atum, the guy who the Egyptian god of Ra is based on."

All eyes turned to Roman. In the silence that followed, Roman started laughing. He doubled over, laughing so hard he couldn't keep himself straight. He managed to catch Brock's scowl and Eve's shocked face out of the corner of his eye, and with great difficulty composed himself. Rosalyn was still staring at him, her lips pressed together disapprovingly.

"This isn't funny, Roman."

"No, no, it isn't. I'm sorry, I'm not laughing because it's funny. Although you should see things from my point of view." He brushed some imaginary dust off his pants. "So you're saying that an ancient pharaoh...what...mummy?...sabotaged my mission to kidnap a Venezuelan cartel princess, had everybody killed in a double cross, went on to co-found a monster Illuminati healthcare PAC, and is now hiding in his pyramid with his tail between his legs?"

Mary broke into a nervous giggle, and Brock redirected his glare at her. She practically slapped her hand over her mouth. Franklin opened his mouth, then snapped it shut and shrugged. "Put like that, he's not wrong."

Rosalyn wearily shook her head. "Yes, that's technically right, except he's not a mummy. That implies death. Thomas King is very much alive. He's very powerful and very old, but not dead. He's from a time before known recorded time, when the supernatural walked with the natural, back when humans knew that monsters were real. He was born from the mingling of our blood with their blood. I don't know how to better explain it..."

"He's Nephilim," Eve croaked. "An outsider. He's demon-bred. His kind consorted, " her face twisted on that word, "with mankind, to produce a creature spawned from Hell."

They were silent. Mary rubbed Eve's back as she struggled with the aftereffects of speaking so much. Roman grimaced in concern at Eve and turned back to Rosalyn.

"What's nephilim?" She wouldn't meet his eyes, instead crouching down beside Franklin, pointing to something on the display for him to adjust. Brock spoke up, surprisingly.

"'Tis the name the holy gave to those of us that were around before the Cleansing. What your kind called the Flood."

Roman blinked, then frowned again. He reached up and rubbed his temples. "Like as in the Bible? Noah and the Ark?"

Rosalyn was fiddling with the controls of the projector with Franklin looking on worriedly, having given up trying to meet her expectations. "To answer your earlier question, Roman, the reason why here, in particular, is because this portal leads to another dimension, to a temple. It was where Egyptian legends say the Benu-Phoenix, an ancient creature of great power, would come to restore itself. It's possibly because of that legend that King is here. He might be planning something, something to do with its power. My sources, the same sources who gave us this breakthrough, told me that he would come here every few decades for months at a time. They can advise me better about what we can expect once we get there. The message I received from them was brief and heavily encoded, so they weren't able to give as much detail."

Mary had been holding back, but couldn't contain herself any longer. "We're going there? After him?" she peeped fearfully. The rest of the group broke into arguments, either trying to get their two cents in or chattering with each other about past missions and current situations. Terra and Hunter were in a heated debate, both shaking their heads, while the rangy denim-clad visitor had squatted down next to Mary. The twin hulks were talking quietly to each other, scowls on their faces.

Rosalyn looked around, not happy at the dissolution into chaos and the sudden tension in the air, and Eve paled as she waved to get Roman's attention.

Brock stood up, and silence instantly fell one by one as he glared around the room. "Aye, we go to him. There be no guarantee of when he'll come out, and we are losing time. Every day he is loose brings him closer to more power. The Robinson Estates, the Ro'Benson Cabal, is on the run now, they are finally weak. They been a thorn in our side for years, and we finally have a chance to bring em down once and for all! It will be a dangerous mission, with potential casualties, but we must go to him. And don't be foolin yeself, he knows we come. He's not stupid. He'll have the best guarding him, creatures that no normal man can expect to dare in his worst nightmares. He is not a normal foe, he has been doing this for longer than any of us know."

Brock turned to Roman, "Ye must be prepared to witness horrors such as ye've not seen, and keep going, lad. We must prevail. There will be no second attack."

Roman stared back at Brock, his words from earlier replaying in his mind. Something he had said had struck him as odd, and he had thought he heard it. Then it struck him.

He studied the leader intently, and Brock met his gaze as if he knew where his thoughts were taking him. Although Roman towered over him, he felt like the other man could definitely overshadow him in weight and sheer strength.

"Your kind. You said your kind." And even as Roman said it, his realization opened up and his memory flashed. Little details rose up from the past two months, inconsistencies that he had turned a blind eye to. Intersections that had gone unnoticed, between him and the members, or between Rosalyn and him. Pieces to a puzzle that now swirled into place to form a pattern he couldn't believe he hadn't seen before, had been dissuaded from seeing before. His mouth opened.

"You're not human." The two men kept their gazes steady on each other. Still in shock, Roman broke first and his eyes swept over the room, taking in all the individuals gathered before him in his living room. "None of you are."

One of the men in the back, the lean denim-clad one, bared his teeth in a feral smile. Eve, horror slowly creeping over her face, shrank away from a suddenly quiet Mary who looked at her with apologetic eyes. Rosalyn slowly rose to her feet as the tension of the room skyrocketed to razor edge. Franklin gulped audibly.

Roman's body involuntarily tensed as he mentally traced a path through the room that would get him to his hidden weapons and get Eve to safety. Brock also tensed, his muscles bulging as his mouth set in a firm line. The subtle movements of hands from all parts of the room shifting to attack positions filled the empty spaces.

Rosalyn's voice from behind him cut through the battle haze that was dropping into place in his mind.

"Don't be an idiot, Roman. These are the good guys. Stand down."

Roman dropped into a defensive stance as he whirled around, his reflexes uncoiling to evade the attack he thought he felt coming, only to find her standing in front of a prostate Franklin balled up in a fetal position, holding a gun out to him by the barrel. It was his, he noticed, the one he had hidden in a secret compartment underneath the entertainment center. Her body was relaxed and her face stern, as she raised her eyebrows at him. She was giving him the gun, giving him the choice. She didn't look alarmed, she didn't say anything else, she just held the gun loosely.

His hand reached up to take it, and stopped a few inches away. He glanced over at Eve to see her panicked and pained struggles and saw the looks on all the faces surrounding him. These were people he had interacted with on a near-friendly and mostly professional basis for weeks. People who had helped him, cared for her, and committed themselves to his fight. He nodded at Brock, and all the tension flowed out of him. Rosalyn flashed him a relieved smile and lowered her arm.

"Thank you Roman. You know my past, as much as I could bring myself to share. I'm as human as possible under the circumstances. Yes, the Black Lotus is not human. Nobody thinks that they're anything more than a common street gang that takes in strays. It's a part of their charm. But they are the good guys. They fight against creatures like King and de la Cruz, against the Robinson Estates. Evil beings that look to exploit and corrupt and seduce and take and destroy. Not all of these...outsiders...are bad. Those creatures, the ones that are the enemies of creation, call themselves the Lords of the Earth, but we call them Unseelie. The evil ones. The ones who deal with demons."

"You are all tainted, abominations and demonic..." Eve's hoarse voice gasped as she tried to pull herself up out of the couch. If she could levitate straight up into the air she would've been crawling on the ceiling by now. Mary leaned forward toward her, her hands making soothing motions to the agitated girl, her face still looking repentant.

"No, baby, the Church has lied to you. It's lied to all of you. They've been hiding our presence and persecuting us all for centuries. The priests and inquisitors have always looked at anything that is not human as being evil. Really, we're just as different as you are. Some of us are good, some of us are bad, and some are just trying to survive in a cruel world." Eve looked at Mary, uncertainty in her eyes, but Mary's mollifying tone seemed to be visibly calming her.

Roman, his mind still buzzing, looked at the group with a new vision. How had he never noticed how unnaturally short and stocky Brock was? Or the strange yellow silhouette that hovered just outside of Mary's body, mimicking her movements like a shadow? The twins Frank and Stein made the Undertaker from wrestling look like a circus midget. Even Franklin, as unassuming as he was, seemed to have a greenish tint to his skin in the right light.

He looked back at Rosalyn. "So there are good ones and bad ones? They're not human but help humans?" She nodded eagerly. He shook his head and closed his eyes. His mind went still as he went deep and looked at the constant picture of the smile on the pretty woman in BDUs. He opened his eyes.

"Okay. Okay, you know what, I can accept that too. It would actually plug up some gaps I've had some trouble with in all this business." He looked around the room again, taking in their relieved expressions and Eve's uncertain face. He smiled reassuringly at her. He glanced at Rosalyn thoughtfully, who arched an eyebrow at him, then looked at Brock.

"May I ask how, though? I know vampires and werewolves can transform...is that how all of you can blend in? And how has nobody caught on that other...creatures exist?"

Brock shrugged as he sat down. He sat on the edge of the chair, leaning forward and cracking his knuckles. "Some have a limited form of transformation, some can use the human's ability to self-delude, but many can't blend in with the humans, and hide themselves away. That is actually who the Black Lotus are. We shelter the misfits and renegades who would be hunted by the humans and the Unseelie." He waved a hand at the rest of the room. "Sometimes that sheltering requires more direct and violent action. We also take care of that part of it."

Roman nodded in appreciation. "I can respect that." He regarded each of the other people, meeting each of their eyes, and smiled at them in turn. "Is this all of us then? We're the strike team?"

Brock scanned the room briefly before returning his attention to the 3d display. "For the most part. I might pick someone up on the way."

"Okay, I need some details on the mission. For one thing, how do we get there, fly in on fairy wings?" He cracked the joke to lighten the tension, but some part of him was half expecting a yes. Mary smiled uncertainly. Hunter outright laughed.

Rosalyn smiled. "Anybody else Brock wants to bring in will meet us on site. And as far as fairy wings..." She held up an unusual-looking key. "How does an Airbus sound?"

Eleven pairs of eyes watched the shadows lengthen around the obelisk from a parked van across the rubbled plaza.

Roman rubbed three hours of restless sleep out of his eyes and checked the clip in his gun once again. They had been parked here for close to two hours, and the team was getting antsy. They were waiting for Rosalyn's agent to show himself. Brock kept assuring them that if King didn't already know they were here, he definitely knew by now, but she would not budge, insisting that getting up-to-date intel was the difference between a successful and disastrous mission. While Roman normally would agree with her, his own patience was wearing thin. And he could feel his blood pressure rising with every minute that passed. He rubbed his temples as a way to calm himself down. For the umpteenth time, he checked on the other members of the team to make sure they were holding up better, but really just to distract himself.

The lean denim-clad rangy man, Markul, was a Russian shapechanger, just like his giant bear of a counterpart, Hunter. Neither one had any weapons or equipment to check, so they took turns dozing lightly on either side of the rear doors. Presumably, they were both skilled fighters in their various forms, but the transformations took a lot out of them, so they mostly just ate and slept when possible. Terra was an awkwardly muscular girl who was usually never far from Hunter's side. She would not have looked out of place on a high school wrestling team. She was supposed to be some sort of elemental, able to manipulate rocks and stone. She was in the passenger seat next to

Brock, who sat motionless in the driver's seat staring at the obelisk across the plaza with a scowl on his face. He had sat that way since he had been overruled on going right in. Rosalyn sat right behind him, headset on and fiddling with a radio as she tried to hear the signal from her agent. He was not exactly sulking, but Roman wouldn't be surprised to hear that Brock was not usually balked. But being obstinate seemed to be the norm for dwarves, as in, real stocky diamond-mining dwarves.

The twins, Johns and Abraham Tercel, were trolls. Creatures with incredible strength and size that had a limited ability to reform their structures and manipulate their own flesh. The two sat in the back of the van now, playing some sort of game with changing finger positions.

Eve was next to him, with Mary beside her. She was still pale but feeling stronger. She had obstinately insisted on being present. She had at least conceded to staying close to Mary. Mary, who was something called a dryad, had changed into jeans and a t-shirt and also had no weapons, relying on her magic to defend her charge. She had already used a semblance of that magic, in combination with Terra meditating while sitting on the ground outside, to determine that there was nobody in the plaza. As he had watched the process, he had wondered how Eve, who had taken the opportunity to take a quick nap, would feel about being watched over by someone she would've denounced as a witch only a week ago. He decided he wouldn't say anything.

The eleventh pair of eyes belonged to a fluffy white housecat that seemed to have adopted the group. It had climbed onto the roof of the van and sat waiting as well. Roman had noticed it at the beginning of the wait, but nobody else had acknowledged it, so he had tried his best to ignore it as well. Maybe this was something else about the fairy world he just didn't understand. He was starting to get sick and tired of not knowing what kind of scene he was in. It was part of the reason he was looking forward to some action. At least, in the field, he knew where he stood.

The journey up to this point had been relatively easy and trouble-free, despite Rosalyn's misgivings. And his own. He knew from experience that all missions had difficulties. So if you didn't encounter any trouble on the front end, it was gonna be a very rough ending.

He could tell Rosalyn was apprehensive about something else though, something she hadn't revealed to them. Her insistence on waiting for the agent was a strong indication of that. He knew she was all about mission specs, but she had overruled every attempt to discuss the issue. Since she was the mission organizer, they had reluctantly conceded. Roman knew it would not last long if the mystery man didn't show up, however.

Even as he thought about voicing his concern, however, Rosalyn's headset suddenly spewed static. The team all perked up at that. Rosalyn muttered into the headset, exchanging code phrases, then nodded to Brock and pulled off the headset. Roman leaned forward to stare out the windshield as Brock signaled for the rest of the team to start to mobilize. Two shadows had detached themselves from the plaza's far edge and were approaching slowly.Without hesitation, they soundlessly exited the van and took up guard positions flanking the van. Roman was impressed with their training. Rosalyn, Brock, and Roman moved forward to meet the newcomers.

The man in front was dressed in a voluminous black cloak that covered his whole body. He had dark wavy hair and piercing blue eyes in an angular, mirthless face. A cross containing a green vial set in ornate silver hung from his neck. He had the dark-tanned skin one usually finds in those whose professions require them to be in harsh conditions. Though he didn't appear to be carrying any weapons, Roman could tell from his gait and his stance that this was a professional soldier, dangerous and relentless.

Roman was slightly surprised to see his companion was a young girl, no older than Eve herself. She was very pale, with vividly green eyes and bright blonde hair that was bound with purple leather into two pigtails that stuck straight out from her head. She had a red pendant with a cross on it around her neck and was dressed similarly to the man but with a red cloak. She did not look like a native of the region. Without the outfit, she would've fit in easily in some mall food court on the West Coast. Roman saw that her head turned to the roof of the van, where the white cat was sitting, and flinched.

The pair stopped several feet away from the team. The man's eyes flickered expressionlessly over the group as they spread out before them. He made sure to note the rest of the group back at the van, and Roman noted that his eyes did flick up, as if looking at the cat as well. The man did not speak at first but bowed his head barely at Roman and Brock before coming back to Rosalyn. "*Aijin*, you did not shade the truth when you said you come for battle. Good. You will need it."

Rosalyn gave him a deep formal bow from the waist. "Amon, well met. I am pleased that you are still able to lend assistance, despite the urgency of your own mission. Speed is of the essence. Do you have any additional information for us about this threat?"

Instead of responding right away, Amon took a moment to look over the group, his eyes searching, assessing. When that piercing gaze settled on Roman, something in his eyes flickered, but then he turned back to Rosalyn.

"It is as you feared, Mistress. Tak has activated the Scions of the Dynasty." Rosalyn swore, and Brock grunted. Roman glanced at them, brows furrowed.

Amon bowed his head, his eyes still fixed on Rosalyn. "Yes. They wait just inside the portal, ready for battle. And ready for you. They have been there for many days already.

Amon looked briefly over at the obelisk in the distance, and shook his head. "And he has started the ritual. It is in its end stages. You must be quick, you must be adept. We cannot help you in this, not directly. We will need to stay outside of the portal to ensure its complete destruction."

He turned to leave, gesturing to his young shadow to follow. Wordlessly she complied. As she passed him, he paused and turned back to Rosaly, who had already started turning away.

"I am sorry, *Aijin*. It has been an honor to toil with you. I hope for the best, but I fear this may be the last time we meet. I will get in touch with my people in the city and send them as soon as I can, but you cannot wait for them. Even as we speak, the sun turns." He bowed to her, then bowed to Roman and Brock. "Well met, fighters for virtue. May we see each other on the shores of oblivion."

As they walked away, the girl glanced back once. Roman thought she was looking at him, but then realized where her gaze was directed. He turned his head to find the cat was gone.

Roman looked back at the rest of the group. Most were grim. Markul shook his head in barely concealed dismay. They had huddled together as Rosalyn and Brock discussed a battle plan. He listened for a few minutes, but they were just arguing back and forth over the same points. They didn't have a true plan, and they were scared.

Eve had pulled out her father's journal and was frantically turning pages. He sidled up to her.

"What's a Scion of the Dynasty, and why is everyone acting like we just heard our own eulogies?"

Eve shook her head, distracted, still scanning pages. It was Mary, who was close enough to overhear, who answered.

"Oh, honey, just hearing the Scions are active is the worst news. When Ra took over the Egyptians, he needed some trustworthy lackeys to rule in his place when he was taking care of his own business. So he took some servants, a brother and sister and her husband who were all loyal to the death, and did horrible experiments on them. He bound fey flesh to them and infused them with demon blood and cast some wicked nasty spells on them. They were reborn as gods to the ancient Egyptians and brought the entire civilization to its knees in worship to Ra."

Eve closed her eyes, finding the passage she sought. "I knew my father's book mentioned them. They are no longer alive but automatons, indestructible and powerful. Osiris, Set, Isis."

"He lists that they have no known weakness."

Roman nodded. "Of course. The party wouldn't be jumping without all the guests of honor." He checked his gun again, then unexpectedly grinned.

"Maybe it won't be as bad as we think?"

It was worse.

Without intel on the design of the dimension, without any idea where the portal would deposit them, without even an idea of exactly what they would be facing, as nobody present had ever fought a Scion but just knew of their exploits from legends...the team knew their only chance was to go in guns blazing. There wasn't much in the way of preparation from Brock. Eve said a silent prayer, asking for help and guidance in the coming battle, and Roman surprised himself by praying with her. He insisted on, and was allowed to, leading the way, his gun drawn.

At Rosalyn's signal, he walked straight into the side of the stone pillar, expecting to walk into the wall. Instead, the view of the scarred stone sort of dissolved into a reddish wasteland whipped by desert winds.

They appeared right at the edge of the original solar temple of Ra-Atum, a giant block of stone plaza open to an unmoving red desert sun that blazed without mercy. In the center was a colossal ziggurat made of obsidian streaked with marble, looming over their heads. Large steps had been cut into the stone on all four sides, leading all the way up to the top, where the small figure of King could barely be made out next to a twin of the obelisk and a large wide stone altar that shone bright red.

The view was slightly obstructed by the three large figures towering over them, already moving to attack even as Roman became aware of his surroundings. He shouted a warning to the incoming team members and dodged the first attack, a stone block crashing down where he had been standing only moments before. They had emerged from the portal right into an ambush. The team immediately split up, dividing the forces between them as they tried to create some sort of opening for someone to go for Ra/Tak/King.

Osiris was a goliath, a giant of a monster, at least ten feet tall and shoulders as wide as Roman was tall. He was haphazardly wrapped in the decaying cloths of the ancient mummies. What skin could be seen between the strips was sickly green and leathery. He wore a tarnished gold crown and torc and swung a massive flail twohanded with an ease that was scary. It was bad enough that the creature was so strong that each time that flail struck stone it shattered it, but it could send booming winds cutting into the group as it crashed into the ground, scattering them and wrecking their initial charge. The only saving grace was that he was slow, requiring precious minutes to recover from an attack. The first time Osiris had swung down on Roman Terra *shifted,* turning her body into rock to deflect the blow, but only barely managed to send the weapon away as it ponderously swung at her. His skin seemed impervious to her powerful blows or the strikes from Brock's sledgehammer. And Roman's bullets glanced off the leathery hide as if hitting tank armor. The three had to dance around the creature, dodging strikes and staying out of reach of the deadly winds.

Set was a white-skinned figure only slightly shorter than Osiris armed with a sickle and a rod. He was emaciated, almost skeletal, but his black eyes burned with hatred as he watched the intruders. His flaming hands glowed with mystical energies as he kept hurling fireballs of black power from the rod at the two shapechangers who kept leaping at him to grapple him. His feet didn't touch the ground, however, his body hovered almost a foot off the ground. He was also much more agile than Osiris, dodging their attacks and slashing at them with the sickle when they got close. The twin trolls had even worse luck, as Abraham got hit with the sickle on the initial rush, and was down. Johns was dragging him away from the levitating Scion, trying to protect the two of them from the occasional fireballs with a piece of stone he had ripped out of the ground, and barely succeeding.

Isis was a lithe, dark-skinned woman of Egyptian beauty dressed as an ancient Egyptian queen and twirling a staff bladed at both ends. She had a golden mask over her face, from which her two catlike eyes peered out. She was impossibly fast and highly skilled at hand-to-hand combat. She was able to keep the yellow wraith-like form of Mary at bay and dodge Rosalyn's gunshots. Eve, holding back because her body was still not fully recovered, settled for using her throwing knives, but Isis was easily able to deflect them away with her ever-whirling staff.

None of the three made a single noise between them, but their attacks were so well-coordinated that nobody could get past them or gain any sort of edge. The silence was unnerving, with the only sounds of battle coming from the Black Lotus, but the worse was the speed, strength, and imperviousness of their attacks in the face of that silence.

Roman tried to break away from the Scions or to get past them to get a shot off at King, but he was repeatedly thwarted there too. There was always at least one Scion between anybody and the center of the plaza. Roman knew it was deliberate, but he could find no way to gain any ground. Brock and Terra were slowly losing ground to Osiris, Set kept the shapechangers writhing with pain on the defensive as even they were getting pummeled with fire and sickle, and Isis was impossibly reducing Rosalyn, Mary and Roman to tatters. The sword of Spees had activated, but Eve was just barely hanging on to it, her shoulders slumped in exhaustion from the few lunges she had tried. Roman looked around for a fallback position, where they could at least switch off and come up with a strategy, but was forced to quickly roll out of the way of a fireball as Set broke past Hunter and Markul.

As the Scion lined up a shot at the distracted Eve, a screech broke the eerily silent battle, and a massive eagle crackling with electricity erupted out of the portal behind him, forcing Set to dodge out of the way. It was quickly followed by an actual catgirl leading several other fantastic creatures. Rosalyn whooped. Amon's backup had arrived. The three Scions paused in their attacks, looked at each other for a split second, and then retreated as one to the area around the steps. The original team immediately fell back themselves, taking advantage of the break and reinforcements to minister aid. Brock quickly took charge and directed the newcomers to various points, focusing on Osiris and Set.

Roman rushed to Eve's side as she reeled toward him, pointing up. Mary, a greenish apparition floating through the air, passed through her and for a moment Eve flared green. Then Mary flew on toward Abraham. Eve took a deep breath and staggered against him.

"He's completing the ritual," Eve rasped. King's movements and erratic gestures were slowing as he raised his prize from up off the altar. Everybody finally got a chance to see that he had a person with him, lying on the stone, unresponsive. Roman and Eve stared in horror as they realized that not only was it a child, but they recognized her.

"NO!" screamed Rosalyn as Andrea's still form came into view in his arms. Roman spun around to grab her but she jerked out of his hands and tried to run to the steps. Isis appeared out of nowhere and swept her legs out from under her. She raised her staff to strike, but was forced back as she was attacked by the catgirl. Rosalyn struggled to get up but Isis was now attacking both of them, and the woman fell back away from the steps.

Roman and Eve had already moved forward away from the two, him practically carrying her. Watching the battle carefully, Roman spotted the gap in Isis's defense and slipped past, reaching the bottom steps. As he started up, gun drawn, Eve collapsed. Though she looked much better than when they had started, Roman could immediately tell that she was running out of energy.

Roman stopped and reached back to grab her, but she pressed the hilt of the sword into his free hand instead. The blade flickered out of existence.

"Go," she hissed and drew a pair of wicked-looking daggers with ivory hilts. She looked away, and Roman raised his head. Isis had noticed they had gotten by her, and was bounding toward them.

Roman, aware of the escalating fury of the fighting around them and the approaching presence of the Scion, debated only momentarily. He was a soldier, first and foremost. He knew the sacrifices that had to be made in the heat of battle. His lips pressed together as he looked down at Eve's affirming eyes. But this might be their only chance, and they both knew it. He nodded to her, squeezed her shoulder, then vaulted up the steps.

In barely moments he reached the top. As he leaped onto the platform, the sword blazed into life. He immediately pointed the gun at the figure who stood before him. They locked eyes for the first time in decades, and Roman noted with renewed rage that Thomas Alexander King hadn't aged a day since that mission. He was tall and thin, with dark red hair drawn up in a ponytail, and small hazel eyes framed by the circular glasses he always wore. His attire today was very different, however, as he had on an ornate royal headdress and a white pleated kilt. A white tunic on which a wide golden torc rested completed the image of an ancient Egyptian pharaoh.

"Get away from her, King."

King sneered at him. "Ah, Roman Capule. The great covert operative. Mr. Super Spy. Or should we drop the pretenses? Let's face each other as who we really are, don't you think, Cameron Paul?"

"I don't go by that name anymore, King. Let the girl go."

"Call me Tak, Cameron, in the interests of full disclosure. And this girl? This one was always promised to be mine. De la Cruz bred her especially for this purpose, for my purpose. That bloodsucker was a fool who didn't know what power is...I should thank you for getting rid of that dead weight for me." He glanced over at the motionless face of the girl in his arms, then looked back at Roman, grinning. "How does it feel to lose another girl to me, Cameron? It seems to be a theme with you."

Roman snarled and stepped forward, but he froze when King dropped Andrea unceremoniously back on the altar and pulled out an obsidian knife from his belt. The stone blade glittered cruelly.

"Stop right there, superagent. You should never have gotten this far, never gotten to this place, but you know what? It doesn't matter now. None of this," he gestured around them with the knife, "matters. You're too late. You're all too late. After all this time, after all these centuries of worrying about you, you're finally too late." His eyes were whirling, and Roman felt a cold trickle down his spine. He had a growing suspicion that King had checked out. Behind him, the sigils on the obelisk looming over the altar glowed with an orange-red eminence, flowing in and out of the air, writhing with life. Roman felt a crackling in his head, and his eyes were drawn against their will to the obsidian pyramid tip of the obelisk. He wrenched his eyes away and raised his gun hand again, then thought better of it and threw the gun down. He distantly heard it clattering down the steps. Instead, he pointed the white-hot sword at King. The crackling intensified, the sword seemed to swell in size, and he noted with interest that King flinched away from it. He stepped forward.

"I'm not too late, traitor. I'm here now. And I am going to kill you. For this girl, for my friends down there, for whatever stupid nefarious plans you have to destroy everything, and for Stacy."

For a brief moment, King looked confused. "Who?"

"Do you remember that mission in Venezuela, the one where you tried to have me killed? The marine who was with me?"

King's face contorted and he cackled. The light from the obelisk recoiled as the flesh on his face bubbled and moved, looking like something was crawling underneath it. "That jarhead? Seriously? She was collateral damage. They all were! You were the one who was supposed to die! You and your rutting charms...you messed up my plans! You were the one who was foretold was going to be the one to stop me and destroy my work. Destroy me. As if an insignificant mortal could touch me!" He threw his arms up, and lightning struck down, hitting both palms. Roman recoiled from the blasts. He blinked away the afterimages, tears now running down his cheeks.

"You may have inconvenienced me in the short term...but look at you now. The Ro'benson Cabal was just a cog in a worldwide plan. The Lords of the Earth will rule over the mortals, and I shall rule them. One step!" he screamed as Roman tensed forward. "One step and I slit this girl's throat. Completing the ritual. Giving me infinite power. All because you chose to come against me. ME!" he roared, spittle flying from his lips. "Your friends will be decimated by my loyal Scions. Your little witch hunter is already dead. Thanks to ME! You've already lost, without a prayer, without even a sliver of hope. By your own doing! When I release the Benu-Phoenix, this body will absorb all of its energies, and then I will kill her, taking it all for myself. You are..."

Lower the sword of Spees, Roman Capule. He cannot hurt us.

The crackling in his head resolved itself in his head into words, and Roman was surprised to find the sigils on the obelisk were flickering in rhythm to them. The fact that words were forming in his head was no longer out of the realm of possibility, and so he didn't question it. Instead, he frowned as he struggled to form a response.

You do not need to acknowledge my communication, Roman. Do not fear. You and the girl are safe. It does not know the power I command. It does not understand what it has done. I will keep her safe. Come forward, Roman. Come to me.

As Roman tuned King's tirade out, he watched the light creep up the girl's feet, resembling ribbons of fire. The voice was gentle and sure, and he was overwhelmed with a soothing trust. He didn't feel there was any malevolence or hostility from the voice, but rather an urgent but loving care.

Faith, Roman. The first step takes the faith of a child. All is as it is supposed to be. You have the heart, you have the faith.

He was out of options. Every way was death for someone he loved, someone innocent, someone undeserving, someone under his protection. He was death for everyone he loved. Eve. Stacy. He watched as King raised the dagger over Andrea's still body.

The choice is yours to make. You don't have to accept the role that you've been given, just because you fulfill the requirements. There are other roles. There are other paths to walk down. Nothing is set in stone. Put the sword down, and come to me.

Roman did the hardest thing he had ever done in his life. He lowered his arms and let the sword's blade blink out.

It was time to take this battle to another level.

He took a deep breath, stared King into shocked silence, and took a step forward.

The obelisk erupted flames as the dagger descended. His own cry was drowned out by Rosalyn's scream as blood spurted out the girl's throat. King's triumphant sneer loomed in Roman's face as he rushed forward to staunch the wound, dropping the sword of Spees. King lifted his arms to the pillar as the flames sprouted fiery wings and formed into a colossal bird made of flames that overcast the sun and plunged the entire temple into flickering red darkness. All action stopped as everybody looked up in fear and awe. King shouted arcane words up at the being. Roman, his hands drenched in blood and his eyes blurred with tears, was the only one close enough to see his face, see it suddenly change from smug confidence to horror. Then the phoenix blazed blue and exploded.

King screamed as he was bathed in the azure fire. He stumbled and fell down the steps away from Roman, bits of him flaking off and burning to vaporous ash as he rolled down. There was nothing left of his body by the time he would have reached the bottom. At the same instant, the three Scions groaned as one and they all toppled over, motionless.

Time slowed, then stopped. Roman glanced down to find the entire pyramid was frozen in place. A pregnant silence permeated.

The blue fire also showered down on Andrea and Roman. Roman watched in amazement as tendrils of cerulean covered her body, not burning, but weaving and infusing and making her body glow. The wound closed up and her eyes opened and looked up at him, so blue it hurt to look too long at them. He fell back as she sat up. She gazed at him softly, then looked around the pyramid.

Thank you, Cameron. It has been centuries since I've been free.

"What just happened," he said to the girl, confused.

Andrea, or the being that was Andrea now, looked sadly down at the carnage rooted in place below them.

This could not have been avoided, but I truly wish it could have been. I am not uninvolved with the world because I do not care, on the contrary, I care about all these creatures equally. But this creature you knew as Thomas Alexander King, or Tak as it once called itself, tricked me and captured me. It used the energies my transformation releases to empower itself for centuries. Its bonds kept me on the edge of immolation, the absolute peak of my power. It is a painful process, one that is supposed to last only moments, stretched out over millennia. Once I was released, once you were able to distract it, I was able to complete the process. It thought it had more control of me. It thought wrong. She looked down at herself, running her hands down her legs, then lifting her hands up to examine them. I have inhabited this body, for now, to protect it from death...although...She cocked her head at Roman in puzzled amusement... Some of the residual energies seem to have empowered you as well. That is not a normal reaction of your kind.

Roman opened his mouth, his mind awhirl with questions, but the being lifted a hand and shook her head.

I cannot hold the sun still for much longer. Already this pocket dimension breaks down without its creator. We must depart quickly. She glanced at Rosalyn, who was frozen in mid-race up the steps. And she needs her daughter back.

Roman hesitated, then nodded. I understand, he thought at her, and we will be quick. But first, will you tell me what will happen to the girl?

It takes me many years to grow back into my full strength. I am eager for the rest. This body will house me for much of that time. I will not awaken unless needed. Goodbye, Cameron Paul, who is now Roman Capule. You have done well.

Time resumed as the blue glow faded from the girl's body. She collapsed into Roman's arms as Rosalyn breathlessly arrived. Roman relinquished Andrea, the now dormant phoenix, into the frantic mother's arms, who started checking the girl's vitals. He knew she would find nothing wrong with the girl other than possibly a scar on her throat. He had watched the wound knit itself shut. Instead, he turned away to give them privacy, and hurriedly started down the stairs, eyes fixed on the scene below him. He grabbed the sword hilt on his way.

Isis had had no mercy on Eve while he had gone after King. The huntress had tried to put up a fight to keep the goddess occupied, but there was no question what the outcome would be. Roman found her body next to the still figure of the scion, the bladed staff still sticking out of her chest. He yanked it out and laid it down next to them, then he cradled her close. An ache he had not felt in years welled up inside him. Though he had only known her a few weeks, he felt a paternal bond with the girl, a special connection to another person he had not felt since he had said goodbye to his brother and left home. He looked down at her face mournfully, recalling the many times the price had been paid for doing what was necessary. He wondered how many times he was going to have to pay that price. He wondered if it was still worth the cost. He reached out with a trembling hand and closed her eyes.

As he did so, his fingertips crackled with the same cerulean fire that had covered Andrea. He jerked his hand back with a start, and then he saw Eve's chest hitch. Quickly, without fully knowing what he was doing, he laid his glowing blue hand on her chest, covering the wound. He felt the skin under his hand knitting itself together, and then the flush of life returning to the flesh. Her eyes popped open and she took a great, desperate breath. She looked around in wide-eyed confusion, and then her frenzied eyes focused on Roman's.

"Wh...what happened? Roman? Where's Isis? I remember pain..." Her hand flew to her chest, but Roman knew she wouldn't find any wound. He was pleased to see the color returning to her face.

"We won," he said simply. He looked up as the pseudo sun continued fading black and shouts of hurry echoed around the temple. The team was gathering up their injured and fallen, and retreating back into the pale reddish open portal. Roman could make out the images of Amon and his disciple standing in the breach, holding the sides of it as it gradually shrunk. Rosalyn was carefully but quickly moving down the steps, carrying Andrea's sleeping body, and Mary was limping up to help her. He looked back down at Eve, ignoring the urgency around him.

"We won today, but there are more of these monsters out there, Eve Strauss, ordained demon huntress of the Order of Tares. Monsters that are plaguing a world that can't handle them as we can. This world can never know of them, nor of us defending it. Plus, we still have to find out what's happened to your father. So what I'm saying, Eve Strauss, is...will you join me in the hunt?"

She looked up at him and smiled. "Let's get them."

CHAPTER IV

Kyoto, Japan

"I don't care how much they want for it, that price is outrageous and offensive!"

The man impatiently waved his hand, forgetting that he still held the dog's leash in it. The long-haired chihuahua on the other end of the pink Hello Kitty leash let out a yelp as it was pulled away from the bush it had been inspecting.

"Tell them the fees associated with that purchase outweigh the cost of the discounts Kabandha is offering," he said frowning as he halted and knelt. The dog licked the outstretched hand that examined her body carefully. Nati would have a fit if the dog was hurt in any way. It was a stupid dog, but her grandmother had died within an hour of them finding the dog, and somehow Nati believed that they were connected. Some of that old Hindu mysticism, he felt, but as a modern man not only did he know better, he also knew better than to point out her quirks. Her grandmother had been a well respected wise woman and seen throughout her village as someone who knew the mind of the goddess and had been a powerful matriarch.

The dog suddenly went rigid. Emon looked down at it to see it staring off into the night, seemingly into the shadowy doorway of a walled garden across the empty street. He looked and squinted, but all he could see was more darkness. This part of the city in the Nanzenji temple district tended to quiet down at night, being away from any major traffic. He liked to come here at night and bask in the peaceful but charged air, like walking next to a slumbering kaiju. There were fewer tourists at night as well, and most other people he passed were romantic couples looking for a few moments alone. That's why he usually volunteered to walk the dog, despite how much he disliked the bothersome animal. It gave him a chance to relax and clear his mind. Plus, it guaranteed him some adoring and attentive love from his beautiful fiancee. He smiled as the thought of her getting ready for bed tonight filled his mind.

Emon shook his head, scattering those thoughts. He then squinted at the doorway. If he tilted his head one way, he thought he could make out a face. He briefly wondered if he should have brought his glasses. No, he was imagining things, jumping at ghost cats in the shadows. He stood up and brushed imaginary dirt off his pants. The dog was still staring though. It was unnerving him.

"Come," he called and pulled on the leash. He started walking again. The voice in his ear was still talking, shrill and apologetic, but he had long since tuned it out. He was starting to get a headache, frankly. Maybe it was this new earpiece, he mused.

"Listen, Carla, it is not expedient at this time to continue this conversation," he spoke into the air. "I am busy and cannot concentrate on the details. Email me the offer and I will look it over tonight. I am skeptical about the details you are giving me, I will need to see it with my own eyes. I will give you an answer in the morning to send to them." As he reached up to hang up the phone, he thought he saw movement out of the corner of his eye and jerked his head in that direction, back to the walled garden entryway. The dog immediately began to bark, annoying him further.

"Hush, Devya! We are not here to...." he froze. The silhouette he had assumed to be a stone lantern had just very obviously moved. A hand raised up and scratched at a spot several feet above his own head. Wide-eyed, Emon scrambled to pull out his phone and turned on the flashlight. He had to tap the flashlight icon several times before it spilled out light, and he swung it up to shine it into the shadow. Devya whined and started to back away, her tail and ears down.

Into the scant moonlight, now outlined by the tiny beam of light shed by the phone, stepped a nightmare. It was obscenely huge, easily towering over the wall next to it. It looked like an oafish wild man, with grotesque folds of fat spilling over the tiger's skin loincloth which was its only clothing. Two long horns sprouted from the top of its head, and its hideous face displayed three bloodshot eyes. In the moonlight, its skin was reflecting reddish-blue, almost purple. Clutched in its vicious claws was a kanabo, a cylindrical spiked iron club. It was barefoot, making counting six toes on each foot easier. Emon's hand flew to his open mouth.

"*Dō shiyō*!" he whispered. His mother had once scared him with bedtime stories of oni, demonic ogres that would leap out of hiding and drag him back to the hell where they lived to be tortured for all eternity. But they weren't real! This was a bad dream! It had to be! It couldn't be. He cowered back, barely aware of the dog cowering behind him. He couldn't seem to get his senses under control or his feet to respond to his chaotic thoughts.

The oni smiled grotesquely and lifted the massive kanabo and pounded it into its other hand. The shadows behind the creature shifted and suddenly filled out, revealing more monstrous forms with horns and claws. Devya gave a single bark. That broke Emon's paralysis. Without a second glance, he whirled around, snatched up the dog, and ran.

He had very little in the way of a plan. He didn't even question the existence of the real-life monsters that he could hear pounding after him. There was no time for that. His father had been a logical man who had impressed on his son that life was only orderly and logical when a man applied his judgments to it. A true sign of intelligence is allowing the irrational into the pattern your mind has created. Thus Emon instantly discarded the useless knowledge that oni did not exist and instead tried recalling all the ways they could be overcome, or at least thwarted. It was difficult to think as he raced for his life. He glanced back to see the monsters still following, but just barely. While he was faster, they were probably more hardy, and would outlast him if he did not act soon. He remembered something about Samnon Gate being a dragon gate, and so he turned toward the Nanzenji temple in the hopes of finding help. When you are being attacked by mythical creatures, was it so fantastical to look for something equally mythical to help?

Devya was uncharacteristically quiet in his arms, staring back at the oni keeping pace with him. He thought it strange the little mutt was not shivering in fear like he knew he should be. He could not spare another moment pondering that, however, as he looked for more mundane help on the way as well, a passing car or other bystanders or better yet a policeman. For some reason this night the streets were empty of all other people. Something to do with the oni, some power they were capable of conjuring up to disguise the devilry they implemented, he wondered? But again, this was not the time to contemplate what-ifs.

He passed under Naka-mon Gate and now remembered that near the temple was a subway station. He might possibly take refuge in there. At least there would be other people. The subway was never empty, even at this hour. He looked back, catching his breath against one of the mighty doors. There were two of them, the purplish one in the lead and a deep red one with one horn. They kept flickering in and out of visibility, and it had nothing to do with the light cast by the streetlamps. Emon had a brief moment of bewilderment. He had truly believed that there were more than just two.

They were still a block behind him, ponderously taking long strides, but implacably coming. Emon was again struck by a near-paralyzing fear, and logically figured it had to be coming from the creatures supernaturally. Devya licked his hand encouragingly, and he was able to look away and face the intersection. To the right was the walled path that would lead to the Spiral Brick Tunnel and the subway station. He started in that direction but stopped suddenly.

He heard the whine of the dog and patted its head. Although he could hear the sounds of bicycle chains clanking and the chatter of people, he couldn't see anything down that street. There were just shadows. It was unnaturally dark, even around the pinpoints of light that were the street lamps. Emon looked forward toward Shōinan Temple, only to find more shadows. To say that this was not good was an understatement. He glanced back and found the two oni were getting much closer. No help for it, then, he thought. He crossed the street and passed by the concrete posts toward the Sanmon Gate. As he passed, he saw the flicker from the direction of the subway station and watched as another oni materialized out of the darkness. Ah, he thought. They were trying to lure me into an ambush. He ducked inside the serenely sylvan pathway.

He knew he was being herded. He could feel it. And that they were able to do this without outcry or hindrance was getting more worrisome. But he still saw no people. There was no help to be had. He and Devya were being hemmed in. And yet, as he scooted quickly down the stone path, he couldn't help but be calm about it. It was the nature of the temple, he knew. He came here frequently to meditate. Of course, it was usually occupied by either tourists taking pictures or other citizens like himself who just needed to touch the spirit within. This was the first time he had ever experienced the full force of serenity of solitude in this place, and the calm it radiated was overwhelming. It was not a calm that evoked placidity but rather urged clarity and stillness of mind. He had no idea what he was doing, but he was not panicked about his actions. He could feel how right it was that he was at the Gate.

He reached the steps leading up to the plaza where the Gate loomed over the trees. He stopped there and caught his breath again. He looked back at the entrance to the pathway. And groaned.

The three oni (the new one was wasabi green), had stood at the entrance for a moment, examining their surroundings and staring at the gate behind him. He was hopeful at first that the rituals and wards written on the posts were genuine and would keep the oni away, but that hope was squashed when they all stepped over the pilings and started down the pathway. He looked around. He could go around the gate, he knew, but for some reason, he felt drawn toward the area under the gate itself. It was not just because it was fixed in his mind as his destination, but felt the aura of safety from it. He ran up the last set of steps under the gate and past the first set of pillars. Here, he thought. He turned around and set Devya down. For some reason, the dog was still as well, almost peaceful. He thought this might be the longest the stupid dog had ever been quiet.

The oni had passed the stone lantern by then, the largest in all Asia at 6 meters tall. The oni came up to its highest basin. Emon almost trembled again. He had thought that in his panicked state, he had exaggerated their size in his mind. If anything, it was quite the opposite. They were bigger than he had remembered. The iron clubs swooshed through the air with menace, and the green oni casually swung its kanabo against the side of the steps as they started up, shattering the stone. And yet he waited. For what he did not know. That calmness that had brought him to this point now urged, no, demanded, patience. He felt like he was hearing Nati's voice soothing him, like after his nightmare episodes.

Thus, he was not surprised when a man stepped out from behind a pillar on the other side of the gate. He was gaijin, a foreigner. American, by the looks of his features. The man was dressed in blue combat fatigues, as soldiers on American television shows wore. He had on unusually bulky sunglasses with a scope in front of the right eye. He was also carrying a large gun he had never seen before. It looked more like a small cannon. Emon was worried anew, and he opened his mouth to say so to the new man.

"Relax, buddy," the gaijin said in English. He shot Emon an easygoing grin, and Emon was relieved to see it. He didn't realize how on edge he had been up until this point.

The three oni slowed down at the top of the steps and squinted at the new addition to this encounter. They didn't seem to react in fright at all to the huge gun in the man's hands but rather looked confused as to what was going on, and what their next action should be. They looked around, puzzled, then looked back up at the American.

"Evening! How's the weather tonight?" The gaijin called out insolently to the trio. Fortunately, Emon was multilingual, as his job required him to deal with the suppliers of many different countries, and he was able to easily understand the American and his easy way of speaking.

The three growled to each other, just barely out of earshot.

"Ah, the strong silent types. Alright, you big lugs. How bout you turn around and walk away from my new friend...ummm..." the man raised an eyebrow at Emon.

"Kobayashi Emon," he supplied helpfully.

"...Perfect! My pal Emon here!" The stranger flashed a million-dollar smile at the three demons. "Or I'll demolish you where you stand!" He cocked a finger at them and winked. It was like he is deliberately trying to antagonize them, Emon thought frustrated.

The three seemed to come to an agreement, because they spread out and started slowly stomping across the plaza, toward the two of them. The stranger shook his head.

"Tsk, tsk. They always want to do things the hard way," he said as he started flicking switches on the gun. Emon was surprised to see Devya walk over to him and sniff his leg. The man peered down in surprise at the dog, then looked up at Emon.

"I'd keep a tight hold on that leash if I were you. This PEP packs quite a punch." The gun started to hum as it powered up. Lights were flashing at various points across it. Emon pulled on Devya's leash and backed up further under the great arched ceiling, and wondered if perhaps now wasn't the time to run like a madman.

The man braced himself against the column, raised the gun at the first oni, and pulled the trigger.

A red beam, pencil-thin, shot out from the muzzle and centered on the creature's chest. Quick as lightning it grew to encompass its whole body, and then the air exploded. Emon didn't know how else to describe the sensation. He felt the percussive winds buffet him as he dove behind a column, and the monster went tumbling down the stairs, stunned and immobile. Its kanabo had simply vanished. The other two turned to watch their companion writhe in pain at the bottom of the stairs. They turned back to the stranger, growling and snarling. As one they charged, swinging their deadly clubs before them.

The gaijin got off one more shot before they closed but it was not as on target as his first shot, hitting the reddish one low and off-center, sending it staggering back to the side. The man then effortlessly ducked the green oni's smashing blow. The club hit the wooden pillar and crashed right through it. The stranger kept the momentum of his dodge going, rolling on his back around the oni and coming up behind it. There was a high-pitched electrical whine and then the stranger punched the oni in the back with his glove. Even Emon felt the shock of the charge explode on the creature, and it howled in pain as it swung around at the now empty space where the man had been. The man was backing away, frowning down at the PEP and fiddling with the controls. He flashed a nervous smile at the oni ominously approaching.

"Okay, now, there's no need to be so irate. We obviously got off on the wrong foot. I brought a sonic gun to a club fight, you brought your buddies, mistakes were made all around. Let's fair this up, shall we? Look, I'll drop the gun, and we can fight mano to mano, capiche?" True to his word, the stranger gently dropped the cannon to the ground at his feet, then put up fists in the air in a mock boxing stance. The oni hesitated, then roared at the American and lunged at him.

"No!" yelled Emon, incredulous. "You fool, shoot it!" Why were American men so full of themselves? Devya was barking again, but this time at the red oni which was picking itself off the ground.

The stranger beamed a toothy grin at him as he kept pace with the creature, keeping out of swinging range. "Thanks, Emon, but we got this. Keep the doggie safe." It didn't seem possible for the man to be able to avoid the club so easily, but he made it seem effortless.

Wait, we?

A hideous scream tore his gaze away from the two and drew him to the foot of the stairs, where the first oni was belting out its death knell. Leaping up the stairs was an African-American woman, no, a mere girl. She was carrying an actual sword, a beam of white light like a lightsaber, and strangely enough, a reddish-green ceramic bowl. She paused at the top of the steps, silhouetted against the flickering streetlamps, and Emon got a chance to see her clearly. She wore dull black dancer's clothing which allowed her to blend into the night, and dark gray tennis shoes. Her thick black hair was pulled back in a fluffy bun on top of her head. She had a slim form, more like a dancer or runner, as physically far from his Nati as possible, but there was a fierceness and unseen power to her movements that somehow reminded him of her.

The girl shook the bowl around her, and something trickled out and scattered on the ground in small bounces, then darted to the red oni, holding the sword behind her. Emon watched with interest as the girl made short work of the creature, slicing and plunging through it as if it was made of butter. She moved with a grace that again reminded him of a dancer, and assuaged his misgivings about her capability to fight these creatures.

Meanwhile, the man was still somehow dodging the blue oni's attacks, easily evading the swings and jumping in every now and then to deliver another shocking blast. The creature was getting more and more enraged by the second and was no longer paying any attention to its surroundings. It was unaware that it was now alone, and outnumbered.

Emon, clutching Devya in his arms, had started inching forward almost involuntarily to watch the combat in awe. This was better than the American-made kungfu movies he so enjoyed. The man was very skilled and fast, but some of his moves almost seemed to be impossible. He would pull away so fast and dextrously that it was like watching a marionette. Emon didn't even notice when the girl appeared next to him. He jumped when she spoke.

"Kobayashi Emon, correct?" Emon nodded. He met her gaze and noted with wonder that her eyes were the most brilliant shade of jade. "Good. That's what we thought. We have been waiting for you. Please stay here, away from the oni. And keep that dog safe. Here, hold this for me, and don't be afraid to use it if you must," she said in a delightfully exotic accent as she handed him the empty bowl. He now saw that she had the contents of it in her other hand. Were those roasted soybeans? A distant memory of his grandmother throwing soybeans at Setsubun popped into his mind.

The girl spun away and completed the circuit she had been making of the duel with the American man, carefully sprinkling the beans as she did. There was now a rather large circle of beans surrounding the two. She studied the circle, looking for gaps, and, satisfied with what she saw, pursed her lips and gave a brief whistle. The man instantly dropped the facade of the battle and neatly stepped out of the circle.

The oni raged and charged at all three of them, but it would not, could not, cross the barrier, as if the beans were a forcefield. It even pounded the ground near some of the beans, hoping to dislodge them, but the force of the blow was absorbed by whatever power was in the beans.

The man sauntered over to the two, pretending to wipe his gloved hands, and looked at the girl. "That'll buy us some time. Now what?"

She turned to Emon. "You are confused and want answers, don't you?" Emon nodded wordlessly. He clutched at Devya, who had gone quiet again.

"These demons were summoned to kill you and take the dog. The animal is actually a powerful spirit, an oracle of great vision and wisdom. Whoever summoned the demons was hoping to use that power for their own gain. We are here to stop that from happening...and also to ask for the spirit's, and your, help."

The man shook his head and frowned at the girl. "Under normal circumstances, we wouldn't be so *blunt...*," he said the word with inflection and a pointed look at her. She just shrugged. "...with someone who isn't in the know about these things. But we saw how well you were reacting to all of this, including coming straight to a holy site where they were weaker, and we feel that you can probably handle most of the truth."

Emon nodded again. When you strip away the impossible, the irrational becomes the rational. In reality, he was somewhat relieved that someone else had seen the monsters. He had feared that his own mind was betraying him. "But who would want to kill me? I have no assets to speak of that anybody would want. And why in such a way?"

The man took off his sunglasses and shrugged. "Are you sure there's nobody who dislikes you, even a little bit? A jealous business rival, maybe? How about suspicious people hanging around, somebody new who seems to have taken an unusual interest in you or your dog?"

Emon shook his head. "My fiancee Nati and I live alone, we have recently moved here. We have a small group of friends that do not change. My occupation is stressful and demanding, but not outrageously so. In fact, of late it has been very profitable. I have risen high in the ranks of my company and have been compensated most advantageously for it. It is possible that it may be a disgruntled coworker?"

The girl's delicate eyebrows lifted. "Nati? Your girlfriend's name is Nati?" she said sharply.

Emon felt a shiver of misgiving well up inside him. "Yes, why?" he said defensively.

The girl exchanged a glance with the man, who was also looking at her thoughtfully. "It just...it may be nothing, but it seems too incidental. Would you tell us about her? Nati is not a Japanese name."

Emon struggled briefly, but he could never resist bragging about Nati.

"You are correct, she is not Japanese. She is originally from India, and she is the most beautiful woman in the world. She is very curvy, with wide hips, and large..." he blushed briefly, "never mind. She teaches Indian classical dance at the center every other night, and she is a wonder to watch. She has long black hair that she keeps tied in knots, and she's probably worried about where I am right now. She is loving, devoted, smart, and very savvy about the performing arts. Extremely creative and compassionate, especially to animals. This is her dog, Devya, who she rescued when her grandmother died, and she believes is her reincarnation."

The girl slowly shook her head. "Excuse us for a moment please." She motioned to the man and they stepped away to converse quietly out of earshot. He saw the girl pull out a worn leather book from a back pocket and flip through the pages, showing the man something written in it. The book looked very old. This was all making Emon very nervous. What had Nati done?

The two finished and came back, the girl obviously displeased with their decision. Her lips were tightened and she folded her arms as the man smiled comfortingly at Emon.

"Okay, Emon, so here's the deal," the man said. "We're going to continue tonight's theme and be upfront about all this with you. I think you can handle it, you seem to have a good head on your shoulders. See, your fiance is not exactly who she says she is. She's a Yakshini. They're supernatural creatures, kinda like Hindu nymphs. Voluptuous, passionate, beautiful, you name it, the whole works. Nati is the Actress, who grants wealth and fame if you treat her right. But the yakshini get very jealous and possessive, and have been known to kill the men they attract to themselves." He shrugged and then grinned playfully. "I mean, they're like the ultimate woman, right?" The girl slapped the back of his head, and he laughed.

Emon listened to this account incredulously, his jaw dropping. But hadn't his fortunes at work started after Nati had sat down with him for lunch that day? She was a true giver in every way, but she did seem to get very upset whenever he spoke of the other women at work. He had had to quit his mahjong club because she hadn't approved of Kiyoko and her flirtatious banter. He thought of this more. "And you think it was her that might have summoned the oni?"

The girl, still glowering at the man, reluctantly shook her head. "According to my father's notes, these types of succubus-type creatures prefer subtlety. A heart attack, a coincidental fall from a precarious height. Not something as gaudy as this. More than likely, it was not her. Maybe an enemy of hers, or a prior victim who escaped destruction." The man rolled his eyes and put a hand on her shoulder. She tried to shrug it off.

"But the important part is, there's a chance that she might be bad for you in the long term, more so than a typical relationship with a clingy A-type would be. Supposedly, if you don't treat her right, she could do something harmful to you, out of misplaced passion."

His logical mind could not help but place this dilemma in a pros and cons chart. He was silent some more as he mentally checked through the columns, then looked at the expectant couple before him.

"I find that I do not care. She is loving and caring to me, and beautiful and sensual, and as long as I have her I have no desire to change that. I thank you for this information, but I will stay with what I know. As my father liked to tell me, 'Only great passions can elevate the soul to great things' ."

"Hey, it's your funeral man. But at least you're forewarned." The man chuckled. "And I don't blame you. You shouldn't give up a good thing just because there's a chance of something bad happening." He briefly sobered, and a haunted look entered his eyes. But it quickly passed as he goodnaturedly slapped Emon on the back. The girl shook her head disapprovingly at them both, then shifted to look at the trapped monster.

"We will dispatch this last demon once we have learned who sent it. They will trouble you no more. And you may keep the bowl. Any soybeans placed inside will keep any oni from harming you or yours. The other two are gone, but this last one seemed to be the leader. It is hopefully capable of divulging the information we seek. It may be a further clue to the trail we are following. Which reminds me." She looked back pointedly at the dog.

"Uh, oh yeah. So, Emon, can we borrow your dog? Devya, wasn't it?" The man was polite, but firm. He was already reaching for Devya.

Emon stepped back, clutching the dog and bowl tighter. "You're...not going to hurt her, are you? As I said, this is Nati's dog, and she believes that it has the spirit of her grandmother in it..." he trailed off as he pondered what to believe now that he suspected her true nature. He looked down at the dog, who had been oddly calm throughout this whole business, watching them as if it knew what they were saying.

The girl nodded. "It is probable that your yakshini knew exactly what this spirit is, and was trying to keep it protected. It would also explain why it chose you, for both companionship and protection. You do know your name means 'guardian', right? This night proves that you are well-named. This may have been your purpose."

Emon cocked his head and a half-smile appeared on his face for the first time that night. "I had honestly forgotten. My father had named me, and my mother liked to remind me that I would one day live up to my name." He took a deep breath, petted the dog one last time, and then handed it to the man.

The dog was still, looking placidly at them expectantly. Emon knew that was not normal. He tried to recall all the stories his parents and grandparents had told him growing up, about spirits and oni. Was Devya really an inugami, a dog spirit?

The girl had sat down tailor-fashion. She pulled out a rosary from a pocket and held it up as she closed her eyes. The man and Emon looked at each other, and he flashed Emon a half smile.

"I'm Roman, by the way. Roman Capule. The girl is Eve Strauss. We're looking for her father while we hunt down a big bad demon queen."

"I am pleased to meet you, Roman. And I am grateful for your intervention this night, both of you." He looked at Eve, who sat still with her eyes closed and her lips moving. "Is she praying?"

"Yeah. She does that when she wants to ask for help, or if she needs clarity on what the next step is going to be. She'll be done soon." He scratched the dog under the chin, then gave Emon a quizzical look. "How are you holding up? I can imagine it's been a weird night for you."

Emon thought about the stranger's words carefully. "I think I may go home and eventually believe I have been having a very lucid dream. This seems to be more real than I can handle."

Roman nodded, considering him gravely. "I used to think that too. I was once where you are now. Don't worry too much about it, you're handling it better than I did, trust me." He seemed to come to a decision. He shifted the dog to his other arm, reached into a camouflaged pocket, and pulled out a strange-looking black and yellow gun with tabs covering the muzzle. He displayed it to Emon.

"This is a tazer gun, the M26C. Be very careful with it. It shoots two probes up to fifteen feet away, which you can aim with the laser sight. The default setting delivers 50,000 volts, which would be enough to take out any living person...but this has an adjustable component allowing it to go all the way up to 500,000 with this dial on top. That'll get about 4 amps through just about any kind of thick skin or armor." He turned it from side to side to present the features. He then put it back into his pocket and pulled it back out in its holster, a black leather cover with a snap-on strap.

"This is a concealed carry holster for it, so you can keep it on you hidden. No need to let anybody know that you're carrying, plus I'm fairly certain it's illegal here. But this is just in case you run into something like them again. You don't have to always carry it with you, but it's nice to have something that can stop them."

Emon looked at the thing with distaste but had to concede that there was now a very powerful reason to carry a weapon. He took the case and extra capsules Roman provided with the holstered taser and tucked them all into his jacket pockets. He would figure out how to deal with the weapon later.

A thought that had been slowly brewing in his mind suddenly found a voice. "Are you two...also together?" He blushed at the forwardness of his question, but it did not feel unusual on this night of strangeness.

Roman's eyes widened, and he sputtered. "Oh Lord no! She's young enough to be my daughter! No, we're just partners in crime together, kicking demon butt and taking names." He laughed comfortably. "But I guess I could see why you would think that, being from here."

Before Emon could process that comment, Eve was standing up. Roman handed the dog to her and walked over to the beans. He had pulled his sunglasses out on the way and put them on again, giving the circle one last scrutiny to make sure there wasn't a break. He had pulled out a dagger with an ivory hilt and another taser gun similar to the one he had given Emon. The oni snarled and tried unsuccessfully to bash him through the impenetrable wall of beans.

Eve awkwardly held the dog up and looked it in the eyes. She saw Emon watching her intently and gave him a thin-lipped smile.

"I actually don't know how to commune with the spirit. I asked the Holy Spirit to give me guidance, but He does not usually sanction such things of his followers."

Emon shrugged. "Maybe you can just ask it? Devya is usually pretty yappy, so she's probably eager to talk."

Eve looked askance at him but turned back to the dog.

"Oh Spirit of the Dog..."

Emon hesitantly interrupted, "Inugami. The dog spirits are called inugami." Behind them, Roman snorted in suppressed laughter.

Eve scowled but corrected herself.

"Oh Spirit of the Inugami, please deign to speak to us this night and answer our questions with your great wisdom."

The dog licked her nose.

Eve muttered something in a language he hadn't heard before. French, maybe? She wiped her nose off with her sleeve and tried again.

"Inugami, we ask you..."

I hear the first time, gaijin.

Eve's mouth clicked close. Emon's, on the contrary, flapped open. He had heard that in his mind!

Devya looked at all three of them, one at a time. *You are fast peoples. It takes too long to remember speech.*

Roman pulled off his sunglasses as the oni dropped senselessly to the ground. He motioned to Eve to continue. She shook off her surprise and looked at Devya.

"We..."

Seek my great and ancient wisdom, blah, blah, blah. Devya is slow to remember, not slow to understand. Ask your questions, gaijin, but you will then fulfill my condition.

Eve pursed her lips. "What condition?"

The dog hadn't moved its mouth the whole time, but now it dropped open and its tongue panted out. *Uh uh. Questions first, then condition. That is rule.*

Eve blew out her breath in annoyance. Roman chuckled. "Let me guess. Inugami are trickster spirits."

Emon furrowed his brow. "According to legend, inugami are loyal to a particular family, like a familiar. They tend to be created by black sorcery."

"A familiar," Eve nodded. "I see now. You are servant to the yakshini," she directed at the dog. It just panted at her.

She pursed her lips. "Very well then. We have an accord. I have three questions that I seek the answers to."

Ask away, joshi.

"First, where is the current location and true identity of the creature known as Lydia O'Dell, former leader of the Ro'benson Cabal?"

Running, always running. I see rage and fear. I see lands of ice and snow under the Midnight Sun. I see giants of blue lined up at the roots of a vast world tree. I see the White Queen astride a multi-headed dragon. I see rippling waves of red ice spreading under her feet.

"Well, sh..." Roman, wide-eyed, was cut off.

"Second," Eve glared at him. "Where is the location of the demon hunter once known as Joseph Henry?"

The dog rolled its eyes around until they were white, as if searching.

Darkness. Darkness and pain. Darkness and pain and an enclosed space. I hear the creeping and crawling of creatures beyond. Trapped under an eternal moon, beyond a castle of stone on the other side of the woods.

Eve winced but kept going. "Lastly, is the Order of Tares still intact in any form anywhere in the world, and how would we reach that form?"

Brothers three hide in the cabin. Brothers three lost their way. Billy goat gruff. Hunters prowl outside in a swarm. The blue river is their only escape.

Eve nodded. "Riddles all, as expected when dealing with the spirits. But the information is acceptable. Riddles can be figured out, we will do so later. Now name your condition, inugami."

The dog panted up at her. *You will leave my mistress alone. You will leave this city alone. You will leave, and never come back. You embody death, and I will not have your infection near my roshi.*

Eve blinked in surprise. She glanced over at Roman, who shrugged and said, "We were debating not overstaying our welcome anyway. At any rate, we don't have any great leads. Those guys talking about a shadow wolf were half-drunk, after all. Plus, doesn't really sound like we have much of a choice here."

He stared hard at Devya. "But," he lifted a finger and pointed back behind him, "we are going to stay long enough to take care of this last bit of business. And I'm pretty sure that'll be acceptable since it also keeps you and your guardians safe."

The dog simply stared back at him.

Eve handed the dog to Emon, who immediately started petting it. She walked toward the last oni, pulling out the empty sword hilt and a twin of the ivory-hilted dagger.

Roman walked up to Emon and stuck out his hand. Emon, surprised, took it. "Good luck, Emon. Stay safe. Live up to your name. Keep that beautiful Nati and little Devya here safe and protected. Most of all, don't let anybody know about any of this that happened tonight. It'll attract all kinds of wrong attention. Take this," he handed Emon a business card, with a single number on it."

"I really don't think there's any need for you to get more involved. But should you need to contact anyone about anything supernatural, call that number and leave a message. There are others of us out there, and someone will get back in touch with you. That being said, now that you know what can be out there, keep an eye out. My limited experience has been that while not all urban legends and myths are real and true to the littlest detail, there's enough there to keep you on your toes."

Emon dropped his hand and took the card. "Thank you," he said, almost in tears now that it looked like everything was winding down. He was exhausted, somehow. He couldn't wait to get back home to Nati. He briefly reexamined his feelings about loving a creature that wasn't human. No, it really didn't matter, he decided, wholeheartedly sure. She loved him, and he loved her. He smiled at the foreign stranger, who had somehow become his friend.

"I am going home to my new life as a guardian to an inugami and mate to a yakshini. I will consider myself blessed. And I am honored to have met you and your lovely...uh...partner."

Roman smiled. "Let's say protege. Or better yet, padawan." He shot Eve a smirk, who had looked back at that with narrowed eyes. He turned back to Emon, still grinning.

"If looks could kill. Now you should get out of here before the fireworks start." Emon nodded and, with one last look at the pair converging on the oni, hurriedly made his way back down the pathway.

Roman looked at the creature still inside the circle of beans, just starting to come to. Eve was on the other side, holding the brilliantly white sword. He pulled out a stun baton and activated it.

"Alright. Let's do this."